An Exciting and Adventurous way to view History

Book Three of the

Saving History Series

Search

Begins

Robert Starnes

Robert Starnes

Published by Starnes Books LLC
Edited by Carpenter Editing Services, LLC

ISBN: 978-1-7325803-6-7 (sc)
ISBN: 978-1-7325803-7-4 (e)
ISBN: 978-1-7347928-5-0 (hc)

Library of Congress Control Number: 2019903882

Printed in the United States of America
First Printing, 2019

Dedication

I would like to take the time to dedicate this installment of the *Saving History Series*, to all of the parents, grandparents, friends, and teachers who have the privilege of being around and getting to know a Gifted Child. As someone with Autism Spectrum Disorder myself, I know how hard it is to make friends, but once we have then, we keep them forever. These Gifted Children can do more than most people, but just in a different way. That to me is what is so amazing about them!

My nephew Jaxson went from non-verbal Autistic, to now low verbal Autistic. By the age of five, before he was speaking, he was spelling words out in Russian, then he started teaching himself Mandarin. Again, his brain works differently than almost everyone else's, but he is also one of the smartest people I know at the age of seven. His parents are the best in the world and never give up on him and always push for him to learn as much as possible. So again, thank you all for either raising a Gifted Child, or are friends with one, or you teach several of them. You all make a big difference in their lives, and I thank you.

~ 6 ~

Contents

Prologue: Council's Invitations Answered

The Council knew this special meeting they have called would have a few setbacks and possible conflicts. This thought was a possibility before they were forced to invite the Royal Brothers of the Embers. Before they were coerced by the Royal Brothers, Preston and Payton, their biggest concern was how to make sure the largest, unknown species, Aquarians, remained secret from all other groups, tribes, and humans alike. The Aquarians have lived in the oceans for so long, undetected, as humans have only been able to actually research twenty percent of the oceans, which the oceans make up seventy percent of the Earth. They know they can trust the Fairley's and Windairians, but the unpredictability of the Embers made them question if any of the others would show, now that the Brothers were formally invited.

The Council has already made preparations for a meeting of five, still hoping that the original three groups will attend the meeting. The Council has received no replies regarding anyone refusing to attend the meeting, which they take as a good sign.

Now the day has arrived, and they will find out if the invitation to the Embers was a mistake. They do not have to wait long before the first of their invited guests arrive out in front of the meeting hall. The hall has a circular driveway with a large Angelic water fountain in the center of it. The first to arrive is Emma, the representative of the Fairley Folk, accompanied by her friend Rose. Upon arrival, the two of them are greeted by the Council, escorted inside the meeting hall, and taken to their seats at the table.

Next to arrive is Travis, the leader of the Windairians, traveling alone. Travis is greeted by the Council and ushered inside the meeting hall in the same manner as Emma and Rose were. Travis is lead to a seat next to Emma, and as he is taking his seat, the Royal Brothers of the Embers, Preston and Payton, make their grand entrance into the meeting hall. They were not greeted upon arrival and are unescorted to their seats. Needing no introductions to the others, they make their way to the open seats on the opposite side of the table from the Fairley's and Windairian's.

The Council leaves the groups inside and heads back outside for two reasons. One is to simply get away from King Preston, and the second is to make sure Fisher, the Aquarian leader, has a proper welcome, if he comes. The Council knows the importance of keeping the Aquarian people unknown to the world, and understands if Fisher has changed his mind, and now declines their invitation due to Preston and Payton's invitation. The Council waits for thirty minutes and assumes Fisher has changed his mind, to protect his people. They then turn and walk back inside the council meeting hall.

As the Council enters through the doors of the hall, commotion between the three groups left alone inside the room is the only thing to be heard. The Council can see his absence was a mistake, walking over to the table and taking his position as the Council Leader. Before he can take control over the unruly groups, they have all come to an eerie quiet. They are no longer arguing and yelling amongst themselves, but merely staring at the tall, green, quiet man walking into the room. It is Fisher, the Aquarian leader.

Here we go, the Council leader thinks to himself, walking over greeting Fisher, then walking him over to his place at the table. Fisher takes his seat, while the others keep their stance and stare, until the Council draws all of their attention to his direction. He asks them all to take their seats and listen to why he has summoned them all here today. To his surprise, they all obey his command, leaving the floor open for the Council to speak.

And so, the Council begins…

Chapter 1

Who Trusts Whom?

Once Ian had everyone in the Sky Lounge of the school, he repeated the story Kayla had told him about Sebastian having a half-sister. He also told them about how he was unable to find any information about this previous child by Sebastian's father. As he finishes, he receives the exact reaction he expected from them, blank faces staring back at him.

"Okay, don't everyone speak at the same time," Ian tries to joke with the group.

"How sure are you that this story is true?" Jax asks Ian.

"One hundred percent true. Kayla has no reason to lie to me. She wants to be back in our timeline just as much as I want her back," Ian stood his ground on the validity of the story he was told by Kayla.

"Well, this is news to me. Who is Kayla and what does she have to do with any of this?" Maria is asking no one in particular.

"So, Maria, haven't you been the person Jax always runs to for information from the Council?" Ian directs his question.

"I would not put it exactly that way, but yes, Jax does receive important updates from me, in regards to anything of concern to the Believers," Maria answers Ian's question.

"And who do you get your information from? If you don't mind me asking?" Ian replies.

"Where is all of this coming from, Ian? Maria has given us some very good and accurate information on matters at hand during our entire trip. Why are you questioning her or the information she has given me during our mission to get here?" Jax is now stepping in before Maria can even answer Ian's question.

"Because, either the information she has been given was not fully accurate, or she has been leaving out information from you," Ian explains to Jax.

"How do you figure," Maria is back to asking the questions.

"Well, to be honest, how is it that no one in the Council knew about Sebastian's half-sister? And how is it that none of you were even aware of Kayla, Kenzie, and Connor, considering Kenzie has some very powerful abilities?" Ian is demanding answers from Maria.

"What exactly has Jax told you about the Council, and what do you think we do?" Maria asks back to Ian.

"From what I understand, the original Council members each gave up one of their own children to create the Believers. This was done because of Sebastian and his continued use of the

Time Keeper. The Believers have been around ever since to help make sure that the Time Keeper remains in possession of the next in line of the Hele bloodline. Now, they were never able to directly intervene by showing the next in line where the Time Keeper was, once it was lost, but they could, however, spread rumors to lead them to it. As far as the Council goes, I am afraid Jax has not told me very much more about it, but I suspect that if the original Council members could give up their own children to create the Believers, then they must have some major power, or control, over others," Ian gives Maria a short, but accurate summary.

"I'm impressed. Jax has given you a very good history lesson on the Believers and how they were created. But it sounds like you know nothing else of the Council. Now that we have cleared that up, would you like to explain why you think we gave Jax incorrect information on purpose?" Maria asks Ian for clarification.

"I don't have to know what you do, exactly, to know that information you gave is incorrect. As powerful as I suspect you are, if you are giving information to Jax, then you were given the information, or you know where to look to find out the answers. So, again I will ask you, how is it that you do not know about Sebastian's half-sister, Kayla, Kenzie, or Connor? I don't mean to be so blunt, but we don't have time to compare notes on what I know about the Believers and what I don't. We need to know about that half-sister," Ian demands.

***

"Guards!" Once the elevator made it back to his floor, Mason yells down the hallway, as he finds the other two guards laid out cold on the elevator floor and the traitor missing. "Guards! What happened here? Where is the Traitor?"

Kayla is still in the bathroom, having just broken off her connection with Ian. She has no idea what's happening outside in the hallway, but she is scared. Scared that Mason has found out the truth. The truth that she has lied to him that there is someone else who is the real traitor.

She is pacing the bathroom floor when the knock on the door comes. "Kayla? It's me, Mason. Open the door please. We have a situation," Mason is not asking Kayla, and she knows it.

Kayla walks over to the bathroom door, half scared to open it, but she knows she has no choice. If she does not open the door, he will get in one way or another. She decides it's best to face this willingly.

Kayla grabs the bathroom door knob and gives it a slow turn. She did not have to unlock the door, because she never locked it when the guard, whose body was used to tell her the story about Sebastian's half-sister, was taken away and Mason left her in here to go interrogate him alone.

Kayla takes a deep breath bergins opens the door. *I guess this is it for me!*

As the door opens, Mason is standing there, looking at Kayla. Neither of them speaks for a few seconds. Mason is the first to break the awkward silence.

"Are you alone?"

"Yes, why wouldn't I be? You just left me here, and it was just us two in here. What's going on?"

"The traitor has somehow escaped. As I made it to the elevator to go down to speak to him, the elevator came up and the doors opened, and the guards that were sent to escort him to his cell were out cold on the elevator floor. The traitor is gone," Mason explains the events that happened out in the hallway.

How is this possible? How can the guard just escape? Kayla wonders to herself before asking Mason. "How did this happen? What kind of guards do you have working for you? You have had them watching my every minute, but I feel if I were in danger, they could not help me. They obviously can't even protect themselves. What are you going to do now?" Kayla asks Mason, with a hit of sarcasm in her tone.

Mason feels her sarcasm and threatens her back, "Do not worry about my guards. They are fine and *will* protect you, if I ask them to. Or they will just report to me your every movement, if I ask them to do that. I think you should choose your next words very carefully because what you say next will determine what orders I will give the guards that pertain to you and your safety." Kayla fully understands exactly what Mason means, so instead of saying anything, at the moment, she gives him a quick nod.

"Now as far as the traitor goes, we will deal with him once we catch him. There is no way he has been able to leave this place. So, he is here, somewhere, and he will be found. I will tell you this, his actions do, however, support your theory of him being the traitor. I'm sorry I doubted your assumption about him," Mason finishes.

"I'm sorry as well. I'm sorry that one of your trusted guards is the traitor. I know you don't trust people easily, so being betrayed by him must hurt you pretty badly," Kayla apologies back to Mason.

"Thank you, but I have a feeling you have something else you are wanting to say."

"I don't want to upset you, or overstep my place, but this is exactly what you did to Alexis. You promised her you would protect me, but instead you turned around and betrayed her and keep me as a prisoner. Now you know how she would have felt if she knew this is what you would have done to her," Kayla tells Mason.

"You made your point very clear, Kayla. But you forget, Alexis is not here, and she abandoned you with me. If she knew anything about me, then she would have known she could not trust me. That means that all the things she told me about her being from the future were a lie. Someone from the future would have already known I was going to betray them, so why would she leave you with me?" Mason tries to contradict Alexis's mission of changing the future. He also wants to make sure Kayla remembers just how she ended up with him.

"Have you ever stopped to think that this is part of her plan in order for the future to change? Maybe she knew of your betrayal, maybe she didn't. I can tell you one thing: time will tell if she knew or not. I have a feeling inside that Alexis knows what she is doing and things will work out the way she plans them to, with you anyway," Kayla snaps back in defense of Alexis.

"For your sake, I hope you are right, but I doubt anything she said is true," Mason ends their conversation, while turning around to lead them out of the bathroom and into the hallway to start a manhunt for the traitor.

***

"So, what you are saying is that you have, or had, a best friend named Kayla, who somehow was erased from time, yet you are the only person who can not only remember her, but also can speak to her? And you want to question the information I have given Jax?" Maria speaks harshly to Ian.

Ian knows now that telling Maria about Kayla is a mistake. Luckily for him, he has a quick fix for this. Ian takes a moment to store this memory in the Time Keeper. This is the first time he has used it to store a memory of his own in it, so he is excited to say the least. He will not access this memory now, but will let it play out to see the outcome, before going in and changing it yet.

"Yes, that is correct. You would think that the Council would have noticed a major change in time, wouldn't you? I don't care if you believe me or not, I know that Sebastian has a half-sister, and I know Kayla is real. If you won't help me look for answers, or a way to get Kayla back, then I will continue looking on my own," Ian states to Maria, as he is turning around and walking out of the Sky Lounge.

Don't worry Kayla, I will never give up on getting you back, Ian thinks telepathically into space, hoping Kayla can hear him.

The elevator doors open, Ian steps inside and presses the button for the library floor to continue his search for answers.

~ 19 ~

Chapter 2

Farmhouse?

Ian has been in the library searching for any information about Sebastian's father for the past three days with no luck. *Why can't I find anything about his life before Sebastian? There has to be more to him. I just have to find a good place to start looking, Ian wonders to himself. I need a break to clear my mind. Maybe that will help me think of new places to look.*

Ian grabs all of the books he has accumulated while on the hunt for anything about Sebastian's father, and takes them back to their proper places on the library shelves. After all of the books are back in their correct places, he returns to the area he has been using to gather his research from the books and straightens up his mess before heading up to his room.

Now that he has cleaned the area of the library he has been using, he makes his way over to the elevators. As Ian is waiting for the elevator to reach the library floor, after he has pressed the up button, he continues to think about Sebastian and his father. Then all of a sudden, he saw a young boy and a man in his mind. They are as clear as any memory he has had before. How is this possible? Ian wonders.

The sound of the elevator doors opening brings Ian back to reality. Ian shakes his head, like he is trying to clear water from his ears after swimming, and steps into the elevator. Still unsure of what he just witnessed, either a memory or just his imagination from all the long hours of research, he presses the button with the twenty-two on it, since he and Brayden share a room on the twenty-second floor.

Ian has enjoyed having Brayden as a roommate for the most part. But after finding out Brayden dream walked him while he was passed out after making a portal from the train station fountain to the school pool, Ian wonders if he still does it without his knowledge. He has asked Brayden if he has continued to do his dream walking, but he has assured Ian he will never do that again without his permission. He said the only reason he did it the first time was because it was an emergency, and he was ordered to do it by Jax. Jax had asked Brayden to go in and see if there was anything he could do to bring Ian back and find out what he could about Kayla. Even though Brayden insists it was only that one time, it still creeps Ian out a little knowing that Brayden can dream walk.

The elevator stops on the twenty-first floor, stopping for someone who is wanting to go up to the rooftop. The doors open and there stands Kenzie.

Ian has forgotten that Kenzie and Connor live one floor below him and Brayden, so he is caught off guard for just a moment. The last time he had seen her was in the Sky Lounge, three days ago, when he stormed out of their meeting upset about Maria not giving him the information he was seeking.

"Hey, Ian. How are you doing?"

"Hello, Kenzie. I am doing fine. I have been meaning to come talk to you about the other day."

"It is okay, Ian. You don't have to say anything to me. I know that you are not upset with me or Connor. Remember, I can read your thoughts, not that I was meaning to at the time."

"I still feel I need to apologize with my words. I am sorry about that outburst. I am not really mad at anyone, except myself. And I still don't know what to think about Maria. Some things just don't add up, like with her being Head of the Believers and not knowing about you, Connor, or Kayla, when I asked her. I believe she knows way more than she is letting on."

"Well, don't let that get to you. Keep going in the direction you are going. I think you may be onto something. If I were you, I would go back to that memory you saw earlier. That seems to be important."

"What are you talking about, Kenzie?"

"The memory of Sebastian and his father you saw just a few minutes ago while you were waiting for the elevator."

"How do you know about that? Never mind, you can read my thoughts. How do you know it was an actual memory of Sebastian and his father? If it were a memory, how did I see it, now that I am only seventeen and Junior is gone?"

"Who is Junior, and where did he go?"

"It's a long story, but he was not from around here, and he was affected by the time ripple Kayla caused when she wiped herself from history," Ian explained.

"Oh, I'm sorry. It sounds like the two of you were close."

"Well, it took us a little time to get there, but yes, we were close in the end. Now why do you say that was a memory and not just a thought?"

"Well, it did not feel the same as you do when you daydream. This felt more real. I am not reading your thoughts right now, by the way, but I actually saw the memory *with* you somehow. I could feel everything around me. I could feel the air, hear the sounds, and even feel the mixed feelings between Sebastian and Jacob."

"Who is Jacob?"

"Jacob is Sebastian's father. That is who the other person was in the memory with Sebastian. Like I said, that was a memory of Sebastian and his father. Didn't you hear me? I read his father's name from Sebastian's mind."

"Thank you, Kenzie, for invading my privacy because you have just given me an actual name to look for. It has been hard looking for 'Sebastian's father' in the library books. Now that I have his name, I have a new place to start looking for information. Thank you again!" Ian finishes thanking Kenzie while exiting the elevator that has stopped on his floor.

Ian could hear Kenzie saying, "You're welcome," as the elevator doors are closing. Ian makes it to his room, puts in his key to unlock the door, pushes the door open, while calling Brayden's name to see if he was in the room. To Ian's relief, he was alone in their room. *I need to get a shower and some rest, before I go back to the library. JACOB HELEN! I never had Sebastian's father's name until now!* Ian thinks with excitement.

Ian grabs a clean change of clothes from his dresser, takes off the Time Keeper and the ring Kayla gave him for his first eighteenth birthday, which will be coming up soon, again, and sets them on top of the dresser. He has not worried about the two being close together since the day Kayla was wiped from history, on his first eighteenth birthday, because of the ring she had given him. Jax said the ring is harmless now that it has served its purpose.

With no more thoughts of the ring and the Time Keeper, Ian heads to the bathroom for his much-needed shower. Ian turns on the water, making sure it is the perfect temperature, before pulling the shower diverter. The shower diverter allows the water that flows through the tub water spout, to be redirected up to the shower head, letting the water spray out over Ian's body.

The idea for showers actually came from natural formations, like waterfalls. The ancient Greeks were the first people to have showers. Their aqueducts and sewage systems built with lead pipes allowed water to be pumped in and out of large common shower rooms where the Elite and Common citizens all showered. The Romans followed the Greeks, by introducing bathhouses. The Romans, of course, believed in taking multiple baths or showers a week, if not daily. The systems the Greeks and Romans created for water and sewage, broke down and fell out of use after the fall of the Roman Empire. It wasn't until 1767, when the first mechanical shower, with a hand pump, was patented in England by William Freetham. That means the original shower developed by the Greeks and Romans was not re-conceived for almost 1,300 years, after the fall of the Roman Empire in September 476 AD.

Now that Ian has finished his long overdue shower, he can actually feel how tired he really is. He hasn't realized just how much energy he has used searching for Jacob Helen's name.

Ian dresses into some comfy clothes to sleep in and heads to his bed from the bathroom. As Ian passes his dresser, he catches a glimpse of the top of it and notices the Time Keeper is missing. Before he has a chance to investigate the dresser for answers, his exhausted body falls down on his bed. He is unable to fight the exhaustion and falls right to sleep.

Ian awakens to the sounds of birds chirping and the sun is shining in his eyes. He has found that he is waking up in the middle of a farm field of some sort. *Where am I? How did I get here?* Ian wonders to himself. The last thing he can remember is taking a hot shower and now waking up in this field. Ian looks down at his right hand and notices he is wearing the Time Keeper and the ring from Kayla. *This can't be a coincidence,* Ian concludes to himself of the fact he is wearing both items.

Ian takes a moment to gather his thoughts and his surroundings. Nothing looks familiar to

Ian, so he is pretty sure he has never been here before. He also knows that he will not be able to access the Time Keeper until he is eighteen, so he is not sure what he is seeing. This gives him pause as he reflects back to Junior, and for a moment Ian becomes sad. He can still remember Junior vanishing right in front of his eyes in a vision he was led to by Junior himself.

Junior came back in time to stop someone from changing the past, which could, and did, affect his present time. Little did he know that it was his own mother, Kayla, he was trying to stop. But, sadly, he was too late. Kayla had already gone back and manipulated her younger self into giving Ian a ring for his eighteenth birthday. The ring, along with the Time Keeper, ended up erasing Kayla from history, which meant that Junior was never born. Once the time ripple caught up to his timeline, it was too late, and he vanished while trying to explain the future to Ian.

Ian chokes his sadness down and remembers this is not Junior leading this memory. It can't be. Ian knows he does not have time to try and figure out why he is here, but he needs to concentrate on *what* he is here to see. Ian gets up from the ground, looks around and can see a farmhouse at one end of the field. *That is where I need to go,* Ian instinctively tells himself.

Ian starts making his way to the farmhouse at the edge of the field he woke up in, trying to stay low and out of sight of anyone that might be looking in his direction. Not knowing when, or where he is, Ian knows that if someone sees a stranger walking through a field, either shots will be fired from a shotgun, or the police will be called. It all depends on when and where in time he is. He knows he should be somewhat scared, but he does find it funny how time really does not change much over the years. Except that if he is too far back in time, there may be no phones to call the police. But there have always been guns, and Ian knows they are used in all timelines since the Time Keeper came into being.

Ian makes it to the edge of the field, then slowly makes his way over to the farmhouse. He is pretty confident he is in the past, because no police have shown up, and no one has shot at him either. Both are a clear indication of the past. In current time, people usually shoot first and ask questions later. So, with no gunshots, he figures he's in the past, or in a very rural area with no neighbors. Ian settles for the past, once he takes a peek into one of the large farmhouse windows. One look inside and the timeline is confirmed.

Ian is looking at a house from the early nineteenth century. He is looking at a dining room with a long table with six chairs and place settings for six. The room also has a large wood burning fireplace and a China hutch along one wall. The dining room has very large windows with very high ceilings. Ian can only suspect the other rooms in the rest of the house are just as large as this room. The farmhouse looked smaller from the middle of the field, but upon approach, the house became much larger than he first suspected.

Ian can see that the dining room is empty, so he makes his way around to another window. This time the window reveals an amazing library of its very own. This was not like the library at the school, but for a private home it is very impressive to Ian. Three of the four walls, from what he can see, are lined with books on several rows of shelves. There is a small table with a large chair sitting in the middle of the room. It looks just like the type of chair Ian would sit in at the old bookstore where his parents bought the Time Keeper, the first time he turned seventeen. As Ian is taking in the amazing view of the library of the farmhouse, all of a sudden someone comes walking into the room.

It's a young boy. He doesn't look much older than Kenzie. The boy walks over to the wall across from the table and chair that sits in the middle of the library. He grabs a book from one of the shelves, turns around and walks over to the chair and takes a seat. The boy settles back into the big chair and cracks open the book he removed from the shelf and begins to read from it.

Ian watches the boy read for about twenty minutes, until he hears a man calling out for Sebastian. This catches Ian's attention. The boy in the chair jumps up quickly, runs over to the book shelf and places the book he had removed back in its place. He then turns and runs out of the library. *Oh, my, gosh! That is young Sebastian! So that must be his father, Jacob, calling his name*, Ian thinks to himself with adrenalin shooting through his body.

Before Ian can find out where young Sebastian, or his father, he is suddenly staring at Kenzie. She is there, face to face with him in his dream. As his eyes focus on Kenzie, the farmhouse and field landscape begin to wash away, like a fresh painting doused with water before it has had time to dry.

"What are you doing here? Why can't I take a few hours to sleep without someone interrupting me?" Ian asks Kenzie.

"Ian, you need to wake up! You have been asleep for two days. This is the only reason I am here with you now, trying to pull you back to reality. So, open your eyes!" Kenzie is yelling at Ian.

Before Ian can say anything, his eyes open wide. To his surprise he is not in his room, but in a bed in the school's infirmary. While he is a bit light-headed from being asleep for so long, he begins to notice the other people in the room with him. He is somewhat happy that Jax, Brayden, Connor, and of course Kenzie are all there around his bed, so he is not waking up in the infirmary all alone.

"There you are! We thought we lost you in someone else's memory forever. Brayden refused to dream walk you. We still don't know why, so Kenzie agreed to go in and pull you back out. Where were you anyway?" Jax is asking questions, while just being happy Ian is safe.

"What makes you think that I was stuck in a memory? Did I say anything?" Ian asks the group.

"No, but I assumed your being asleep for two days has to be connected to the Time Keeper, thus leading to the conclusion of a memory," Jax replies. "Is that not the case here?"

"I'm not exactly sure where I was, but I have some idea of when I was. I'm also pretty sure you won't believe me when I tell you," are Ian's only words to the group, before looking at Kenzie and thinking, *What happened? Please, don't tell anyone what you saw. Not until we can figure out what that was. Promise?*

Kenzie looks at Ian and thinks back to him, *I promise.*

Chapter 3

Jacob Helen?

Ian refuses to stay in the infirmary, once he is awakened by Kenzie. Without telling anyone *when* he was or what he or Kenzie saw, Ian just asks if he can be released to go back to his bedroom. Ian is not ready to share the information of going back and seeing Sebastian and his father. Thankfully no one said a word against his request.

Ian slowly sits up, throws his legs over the side, slid forward and eases off the edge of the bed to try to stand. He does not want to rush getting up, not after being asleep for two days. He knows if he rushes it and falls down, they will not let him leave the infirmary. *Slow and easy,* Ian thinks to himself.

Yes, slow and easy, replies Benzie to Ian's thoughts.

Kenzie! Can you do me a favor? Give me about thirty minutes to get to my room, then find an excuse to leave the group and come up to my room. We need to talk about what happened, Ian requests of Kenzie with his thoughts.

You got it. I can always find a way to leave the group. They never really ask me what I'm doing anyway. I think it's because I'm still a kid. I'll see you in thirty minutes, Kenzie finishes their conversation.

Ian makes his way out of the infirmary, slowly, and steadily away from the others, leaving them standing next to bed he was asleep for two days. Still, not one of them had one word to say in regards to Ian leaving the infirmary.

He reaches the elevators and presses the call button, then waits only a few minutes for the elevator to make its way to the floor he's on. Once the elevator makes it to the infirmary floor, Ian makes his way slowly into it before the doors close on him. As the doors close, he presses the button for the twenty-second floor. He would like a few minutes to himself to freshen up before Kenzie arrives. He can only imagine how he must look, after being in a bed for two straight days.

As Ian feels the upward motion of the elevator, he tries not to think of anything. He is afraid that if he thinks of anything, he will either get Kenzie popping into his head, or end up stuck in another memory for two more days. Neither of these are acceptable to Ian right now. He decides to focus on the subtle sounds of the elevator, the soft noise the screen makes as it changes from one floor number to the next, the hum of the belts moving and tightening to pull the elevator up, to what he knows will be a loud 'ding', once he reaches his destination. The elevator stops on his floor, with the anticipated 'ding', the doors open, and he makes his way out through the doors as quickly as he possibly can, so he can begin his way to his room door.

Ian takes ahold of his bedroom doorknob, gives it a quick turn and finally he's back in his room. The first place Ian heads is to his dresser. He may have been asleep for two days, but he remembers the Time Keeper being missing when he passed out. Upon inspecting the top of his dresser, he finds the Time Keeper is in the same place he left it before he took a shower. But he notices Kayla's ring is missing. *How is this possible? I'm sure they have something to do with what has happened. How can the Time Keeper be here and the ring not be? Where is the ring Kayla gave me?* Ian is beginning to question his own sanity. Before he can even freshen up a little, there is a knock at his door.

"Just a minute!" Ian shouts towards the door. He's pretty sure it's Kenzie, but just in case it's not, he still wants to be polite. Ian makes his way over to the bedroom door and opens it to see Kenzie standing there with a big grin on her face.

"Why didn't you just tell me it was you instead of making me come all the way over here to let you in?" Ian questions Kenzie.

"Well, I figured I would give both of our minds a break for the day," Kenzie replies with a smile.

"Very funny! Come in, please. We have a lot to talk about," Ian tells Kenzie. "What happened to waiting for thirty minutes so I could freshen up?"

"I just thought that since you passed out when you just got out of the shower, you probably didn't really need one now, since you were just sleeping for two days. It's not like you were running a race for two days, so what's to freshen up?" Kenzie makes her way into his room and takes a seat at a small table in the middle of the room that he shares with Brayden, and waits for Ian to take the other seat so they can start their talk.

"Well, just so you know, sleeping or not, I still like to be clean. Now that you are here, let's talk," Ian confesses to Kenzie. "Oh, by the way, we will not be giving our minds a break today, I hope you don't mind?"

***

Kenzie and Ian have been able to compare notes on what he saw while he was asleep for two days, before Kenzie joined him, and what was happening with the group while he was out.

To save some time, Ian allows Kenzie into his mind so she can see and feel exactly what he did while he was stuck in the memory. It does not take her very long to go through the entire memory. "This is so much easier than having you explain two days of sleep to me," Kenzie jokes with Ian.

"I'm glad I don't have to explain every detail to you either. This is way easier, and plus if there is something I forget, you will now be able to remind me. Or at least you will now have a full account of the memory and know everything I saw and felt for the entire two days," Ian replies to Kenzie joke. "And thank you for not telling anyone that you figured out Sebastian's father's name, even if it was by accident," Ian expresses to Kenzie.

"Like I said before, they don't really pay much attention to me or Connor. I guess they think because we are younger, we don't know much. Oh, how they are wrong," Kenzie says to Ian laughing. "I know way more than they can even THINK of."

But to Kenzie's last statement, there is not much that she can share with Ian about Maria or the group. The same reason they pay no attention to her and Connor, is the reason they also use to not include her in anything as well, it's all because of her being young.

The two of them decided that the best plan of action would be for them to come up with what books they should start looking in, and what time period for Jacob Helen. They want to make searching for him to be as quick as possible, because once they head down to the library to begin the actual search for Jacob Helen, they will not have much time on their own, so they need to make every minute count.

A week has passed since they were able to catch up, using the mind melt method with Kenzie, and now have been spending a lot of time together in another section of the library. Now that Ian knows Sebastian's father's name, Jacob Helen, they have been able to do more research on him. Ian needs to know as much as possible about Jacob, before Sebastian's birth, if he wants to find out about Sebastian's half-sister.

Ian and Kenzie both search through every book that has a reference to Jacob Helen in it at the time of Sebastian's birth. They even went so far as to check under Jacob Hele, which is the true spelling of Jacobs ancestors last name, before it was changed over the years, like many names were done over the centuries. But there is nothing of another woman or child in anything they read came up for either spelling of Jacobs's last name, Helen or Hele. "What are we missing?" Ian asks Kenzie.

"If I knew what we were missing, then it really wouldn't be missing, would it?" Kenzie jokingly replies to Ian.

"This is no time for jokes. Why do you always have to make a joke about something I say? But I will say this, when you're right, you're right, and you are … correct. I bet you thought I was going to say 'right' didn't you?" Ian jokes back with Kenzie.

"Ha. Ha. Ha. If I really wanted to know what you were going to say, I could have just read your thoughts. All joking aside, have you ever tried to access one of Jacob's memories? Since he is Sebastian's father, he would have had access to the Time Keeper before Sebastian. I mean, now that you know his name," Kenzie replies to Ian, ending the jokes.

"I can't actually access the Time Keeper until I turn eighteen."

"But you accessed it the other day and even before then, remember? You were stuck in that last memory for two days, but you still accessed it."

"I am still not certain that I am the one who actually accessed those memories. If I did, I don't know how I did it. And if I did, you saw what happened with the last memory I may have accessed. I was stuck in it for two days, and you had to bring me back out of it. I'm not trying to go back to the infirmary again."

"You have a point there. But since you somehow accessed the Time Keeper, either with someone's help or not, you may just have the ability to actually access it on your own. Then again, I guess you shouldn't try that again unless you know you are able to bring yourself back," Kenzie finishes with that topic.

***

Ian begins to spend all of his spare time in the library. He has become more obsessed with finding out about Sebastian's father. Ian goes through every book he can find that mentions Jacob Helen. He is determined to find out his history before Sebastian's birth. He has become so obsessed that he has even went back through the same books he and Kenzie have already went through just days before.

Kenzie has joined Ian with his research, since she has also seen what Ian has seen about Jacob Helen. Kenzie is also keeping Ian updated on everything else that is happening at the school that he is missing, while being in the library and avoiding Jax, Brayden, and Maria.

Ian has been avoiding Jax, Brayden, and Maria at all costs because he is not in a trusting position at the moment. The only person he trusts right now is Kenzie. He trusts her because she has been in his mind and saw what he did and she was able to bring him back out of the memory he was trapped in for two days. He knows he has to trust someone, so for now, it will just be Kenzie and himself working on finding out about Jacob Helen. At least until they find something about him before

Sebastian was born, then he may seek out help from Jax. But so far, they have not been able to find out anything about Jacob before Sebastian.

"We have to find something soon, or we will have to let others in," Kenzie tells Ian. "We can't keep going over the same books we have already been through and expect different answers."

"I know, but I think if we have a little more time, we will find what we are looking for."

"But we don't know what we are even looking for. We may have already found it and not even know it, because we don't know that it is important."

"I know Kenzie, but we just have to keep trying!"

"You know Jax is not going to stay away much longer. He has already given us a week without bothering us, but he won't go much longer until he starts demanding answers."

"You're right. But until he does, let's keep looking," Ian tells Kenzie. "There is something here, in these books and we just have to find it. And if it is not in these books, then it has to be somewhere here in the library."

***

Jax has left Ian alone to continue his search for records on Sebastian's father for about a week now. He has not wanted to put pressure on Ian, in his current state of trust issues regarding Maria, but today Jax decides it has been long enough. Jax has also taken notice that Ian is spending more time with Kenzie, more than before, since she went into his mind to bring him back from being stuck in a memory for two days.

She has to know something that Ian is not telling me. I need to get Kenzie alone, so I can speak to her. But how? Jax thinks to himself. He is not expecting what happens next.

I promised Ian I would not say anything, so if you want to know what Ian is doing, you will need to ask him yourself, is a reply from Kenzie into Jax's mind.

Kenzie? What are you doing listening to my thoughts? If I remember correctly, we had a conversation about this type of invasion of privacy, Jax thinks back to Kenzie in a harsh tone.

I wasn't listening to your thoughts until I felt you thinking of asking me something. I figured if you were going to ask me something anyway, it would be fine to go ahead and answer you in your mind, Kenzie replies back.

Well, you would be mistaken. Just because I was thinking of asking you something, doesn't mean I was going to ask you. Therefore, this is an invasion of my privacy. Please, refrain from going into people's heads, unless they call for you, that is. Is that understood? Jax expresses to Kenzie as a teacher, not a friend.

Yes, you have made it very clear. I will let you go back to thinking of something else now, Kenzie replies, as she breaks off her connection with Jax.

Even though Jax is upset with Kenzie for interrupting his thoughts, he knows she is right about who he needs to speak to. Jax has to go directly to Ian if he wants to find out what he is doing or how his search is coming along. It's time he and Ian start working together, not alone, is where Jax's mindset is now.

Jax decides to go find Ian and ask him what he can do to help. He truly does not want to stop

Ian from looking for Sebastian's father, and just wants to help. He has a feeling Ian is in the library, but what part is the real question since the library is so huge.

Chapter 4

Trust Jax?

"Sir, we have searched every inch of this place and have found no sign of the escaped traitor. He must have found a way out of the building before anyone noticed he was on the loose," one of Mason's head guards informs him on the search's progression.

"Keep searching anyway! I want him found *alive*," Mason orders back as he turns around to face Kayla.

"Why are you looking at me that way? What do you think I could have done, since I have been with you the entire time," Kayla questions Mason's stare.

"Is there anything about your conversation with the guard that you may have forgotten about or left out by mistake?"

"No. I told you everything that happened in the restroom and everything he said to me. All he said is that he has been watching Ian and myself for some time now, and that I was to go with him if I wanted to see Ian, but I started screaming instead of going with him. Remember? If I was trying to keep anything from you, I would have trusted him and left with him, but I didn't. That should tell you who I trust around here," Kayla replies.

"It's true that you did shout at the guard, but that does not mean your version of the events that happened between the two of you are accurate. I'm sure you understand why it is important for me to verify said events, don't you?" Mason asks Kayla without wanting an answer. The two have been walking the halls helping with the search for the missing traitor, ever since Mason first questioned Kayla in the bathroom. The bathroom she had accused an innocent guard of being a traitor in order to protect herself and her mysterious new friend.

Kayla answers back anyway. "Yes, you don't trust me because I'm your prisoner. You can think what you want. I know what happened, and what I told you is the truth. Believe me or not, that is completely up to you."

One of Mason's looks to Kayla was all she needed from him to remind her of his power over the group of his followers. She knows he can make her life worse than it is now. She knows it will be best to be quiet.

"Why don't you go back to your room for the rest of the day? I think we can manage the search without you or your theories," Mason tells Kayla, although it is more of an instruction to the guard that is standing next to her.

The guard turns his body towards Kayla, while extending his right arm out for her to lead the way to her room, and he would follow behind her. The hint was taken, and Kayla did exactly what was expected of her. *Finally, some time alone,* she thought to herself with a small smile as she continued her way to her room.

After about a five-minute walk through the building's hallways, Kayla, with her guard in tow, reaches her bedroom door. She makes a quick stop, as she knows the routine the guard must perform before she can enter her own room. The guard must go in and check to make sure the room is empty, even more so now with the escapee missing.

The guard opens her bedroom door slowly, walking in while looking on both sides of the entry. Once inside, he continues his inspection of her room by checking in the closet across the room, near the one window to the outside. Next he checks under her bed, then begins his way back to the door to inform Kayla it is clear, but before he can speak, she is already speaking.

"I doubt he is going to come back to try and talk to me again, since I am the reason he was caught in the first place," Kayla mocks the guard for doing his duty.

"I have my orders, and I must follow them," replies the guard matter of fact. "I'm sure you understand."

"Well, excuse me. Would you like me to start screaming for Mason, so I can let him know how rude you were just now? Remember what happened to the last guard I yelled at," Kayla takes a step forward towards the guard so she can look him in the eyes. "Now, is my room clear, or do I need to stand out in the hallway the rest of the night?"

"No ma'am. I mean, yes ma'am. I mean, yes, your room is clear, and no you don't have to stay in the hallway anymore. You may enter your room now. Also, I would like to apologize for my rudeness earlier. I meant no offense," the guard says to Kayla in an attempt to keep her calm. He for sure does not want to end up missing like the last guard that Kayla yelled at did.

"Thank you," Kayla expresses to the shaken guard as she passes him on her way into her bedroom. She quickly closes the door behind her. As the door shuts, she is feeling a rush inside of her that she has never felt before. It's more of a temptation compelling her to be mean again.

That was more fun than I expected it to be. Now I see why Mason enjoys it so much, Kayla thinks to herself. *This must be what real power over people feels like.*

"What am I thinking? This is not me, nor is it someone that I want to become. I am a good person. Mason is not," Kayla defines herself out loud. "I wonder how Ian is doing on finding any information about Sebastian's half-sister."

Ian? Are you there? Kayla thinks into space, but receives no reply from Ian. *Ian, I could really use a friend right now. Where are you?*

With her pleas to Ian going unanswered, Kayla decides she might as well lay down and take a nap. The day is early, and she has no idea how long she will be locked in her room this time.

Maybe, just maybe, I can reach Ian while I am asleep, she thinks to herself this time. She takes her place on her bed, gets comfortable, and falls asleep.

***

"Just so you know, I know Jax is on his way up here to find you," Kenzie tells Ian.

"How do you know this information?"

"Well, let's just say I felt him thinking of me, so I slipped into his mind for a minute or two. I heard something I shouldn't have heard, and then I got caught by Jax. I told him that if he has any questions for you, he needs to ask you directly and not to ask me," Kenzie replies to Ian a bit skittish.

"You did WHAT? Why in the world would you go snooping into Jax's thoughts? You knew as soon as you did that he would come looking for us," Ian scolds Kenzie.

"Like I said. I felt him thinking of me first. He was thinking of a way to get me alone to ask me what you were doing. I simply chimed in and told him that if he wanted to know anything you were doing, then that would need to be something that he asks you directly, because I will not say anything," Kenzie explains her actions in more detail to Ian.

"Fine then. How long do we have before he gets here?" Ian asks Kenzie.

"How would I know that? It's not like I have a GPS on him. When he told me to get out of his mind and to stop reading his thoughts, I did. That was about thirty minutes ago," Kenzie tries to give some sort of a timeframe to Ian.

Just about the time Kenzie finishes her monologue about Jax, the elevator door bell rings. This indicates to Ian and Kenzie that someone just reached their floor and is getting off the elevator on the library's floor. Ian figures it must be Jax, based on the small window of time Kenzie had given him. Ian decides to go meet him, instead of having Jax search the entire library for them.

"Stay here! I will go get Jax and see what it is he is actually wanting to know. I'll be right back," Ian tells Kenzie as he turns to leave the row of books they have made their central hub for research.

Ian makes a scurry down a few rows of books, away from their hub, before calling out to Jax. He is not ready to give up his work location to Jax just yet.

"Jax? Is that you?" Ian asks loudly, even though he is in a library.

"Yes, Ian. Where are you? I would like to speak to you for a few minutes. If that's okay with you," Jax shouts back just as loud as Ian did.

Ian is coming around the corner of the elevators just as Jax finishes his loud reply.

"Shush, we are in a library don't you know?" Ian says to Jax with a short giggle in his voice.

"Very funny, Ian. Laugh all you want, but you were talking just as loudly as I was," Jax tells Ian.

"Yes, but I am a student and you are a teacher. I think more is expected from the faculty than the students here at the school, don't you?" Ian smirks back.

"You have made your point. Now can we be civilized for a few minutes? I only came up here to ask if there is anything I can do to help you with your search," Jax clarifies to Ian.

"What makes you think I am doing anything that requires help?"

"I know you have your reservations on trusting Maria, but let's put that aside for the moment. I know you are searching for Sebastian's half-sister, and I want to help. I know you and Kenzie are up to something. I want to be here to make sure that whatever it is, you are safe," Jax explains to Ian.

"Fine, but if I let you help us, you will at least have to listen to our ideas before shutting them down. And by no means are you to tell Maria, or anyone else, about what we are doing. Are you okay with that?" Ian asks Jax for conformation on his loyalty.

"I will make you a promise that I will not tell Maria, or anyone else, unless it's an emergency situation, and I deem it necessary to inform someone. Remember, I am a teacher here, and I do have responsibilities to the school, students, and even to the Council. Is that something you can agree with?" Jax expresses his concern to Ian.

"It depends on what you would consider an emergency. Would you tell me first before you inform anyone else, or would this begs done behind my back?" Ian questions Jax's motives.

"I will never go behind your back, Ian. The only way you would not be included in the decision to decide if it's an emergency or not, would be if you are unable to join in the discussion, you know, like being stuck in a memory, or dream you can't get out of by yourself," Jax reassures Ian.

"Well, that does sound fair and like it would be an emergency situation. If those are the types of circumstances you are talking about, then that is something I can agree with," Ian settles things up with Jax. "You can help us then. But just so you know, we have gotten nowhere so far with the search for Sebastian's half-sister."

Ian fills Jax in on everything he and Kenzie have found out so far, which has led them nowhere. Ian also briefs Jax on Kenzie's idea of him trying to access the Time Keeper, even though he is not eighteen yet. Ian is a bit surprised that Jax did not say anything about it not being possible. This struck some interest within Ian. *Maybe it is possible for me to access the Time Keeper at seventeen,* he thinks to Kenzie.

I told you it might be possible. But just like everyone else, you don't listen to me because I am just a kid, Kenzie thinks back to Ian with a small hint of laughter.

You know that's not true at all. There is no need to joke about that. You and Connor are the only people I can fully trust right now, so don't start thinking I am the same way the others are. Please? Ian pleads back to Kenzie.

Okay, no more jokes. I know you listen to me and trust me. Don't worry, I'm not going anywhere. So, what are we going to do now? Now that Jax is going to be helping? Kenzie thinks back.

I'm not sure yet, but I think we may be trying something soon. We will see, are Ian's last thoughts back to Kenzie before giving Jax a look of interest.

"Did you know that libraries first appeared over five thousand years ago, in the area that ran from Mesopotamia to the Nile in Africa, called Southwest Asia's Fertile Crescent? This place is also known as the birthplace of writing. Many of the records that were found in the archives here mark the end of prehistory and the start of history.

Many of the earliest forms of writing were done on clay, or mud, tablets around an inch thick in various shapes and sizes. Mud was poured into a wood frame, smoothed out then allowed to dry until it was damp. Once it was damp, they would write on the soft mud. When they were finished writing what they wanted to record, they would then let it finish drying out in the sun. Now, if they needed it to dry quicker for some reason, or another, they would dry them in a kiln.

One of my favorite parts of this lesson is finding out that they would stack their written work side by side with the wood frame facing out, and they would write the title of their work on the wood, so it could be found easily by others. It is just about the exact same way as we place books on the bookshelves today, and how authors place the titles alone the spin of their novels," Jax spills out facts about the library. He can't help it, being a history teacher and all, when the opportunity arises a lesson, he tries not to pass them up.

Chapter 5

Mirrors?

"Look, I know you want to go back to Mason and tell him everything you know, or at least think you know, but you can't ever go back. I know you may have had no control over your body, but you do remember what everyone else back at the group thinks *you* did, not me. So, you see why you can't go back. You have been accused of being a traitor. With your escape now, you look more like the traitor than before. If you try to go back, Mason will have you locked up in the basement forever, and he will never believe a word you tell him. He will think you are crazy. So, if you want to live a long and free life, once I release control of your body back to you, you will run and run and never look back," the escaped guard is telling himself, while looking in a mirror at a gas station bathroom, about six miles away from Mason's base.

"You know what I am telling you is the truth. You know Mason better than most people, and you know what he will do to you. I am sorry I did this to your life, but this was a risk I had to take. If it helps to fix history, then none of this will even matter to you, and you will get your old life back. I promise," are the last words the guard speaks to himself in the bathroom mirror before gaining control over his own body again.

"What kind of mirror is this? It must be some kind of trick mirror, like you see at a carnival, because there is no way I just had a conversation with myself," the confused guard thinks out loud while curiously inspecting the mirror.

Mirrors go back over 6,000 years. The earliest mirrors were found in Turkey. The Turkish mirrors were made of polished stone and black volcanic glass obsidian. The Ancient Egyptians used polished copper, while Ancient Mesopotamians procured metal mirrors, and stone mirrors were used in Central and South America from about 2000 BC. It is believed that mirrors made with metal backs and glass were first produced in Lebanon, in the first century AD, while the Romans made crude mirrors from blown glass with lead backs. In 1835, a German chemist invented a way to help mass produce mirrors, so then anyone could afford to buy a mirror.

There are many stories of mirrors holding superstitions, but none involve talking back to oneself. Unless you include fairytales, then you can include the mirror in Snow White, because that mirror spoke, but only to the Queen. The superstitions were more about having seven years of bad luck if you broke a mirror, as old Roman legend says it takes seven years for a person's soul to regenerate. Other stories are how the devil can trap the soul of the dead in the mirrors, unless they are covered up once someone dies. Or the superstition if a mirror falls off a wall on its own, means someone you know is going to die. Still none of these involve talking mirrors. It is said that if you bury all the broken pieces of the mirror deep into the ground as soon as it happens, you can avoid seven years of bad luck, but it must be every piece.

The guard has no choice but to believe what he does not understand and run for the rest of his life. So that is the last time the escaped guard is ever near Mason or his group. He just vanishes into the world of regular people.

Back at Mason's basecamp, the mysterious history student is back in the body he has been assigned for this time period. "I hope that is enough to get history back on its correct path," he says out loud to himself.

"I need to get back to my lessons if I want to pass this class and if I want to see if anything I have done has set history back on its true path. Also, I need to check on Kayla and see how she is doing."

***

Now that Jax is helping Kenzie and Ian, his first suggestion is to take a break from the school and the library. He insists that they go shopping so they can go back to the library with a fresh set of eyes and clear minds. He told them that this may open up new paths for them to pursue for Sebastian's half-sister. So they take a car down to Kirby Dr. and hit some stores.

"I say we at least try it," Kenzie tells Jax. "You are here, so what do we have to lose?"

"It's not that simple. There is a lot of planning that goes into these things, and I feel you are rushing me. Give me a minute to think of this one first," Jax asks of Kenzie.

"You two need to make up your mind, or I will make the decision for all of us," Ian chimes in.

"Fine then. You win. Let's do it. But if I change my mind, then I get to bring it back. Deal?" Jax asks of Kenzie and Ian.

"Yes, if you don't like this bedding set for your room, you can bring it back. But I think this one suits you the best," Ian tells Jax, as they stand in the middle of Bed, Bath and Beyond. *You would think this is the first time Jax has ever bought himself a bedding set before,* Ian thinks to Kenzie.

With that, Kenzie starts laughing out loud, right in front of Jax and the entire store. She is laughing so hard that everyone around her beings to stare at them.

"What is so funny Kenzie?" Jax asks. "What did you say to her Ian?"

"I have not said a word to Kenzie. You have been standing right here with me. Have you heard me say anything?" Ian replies to Jax with a laugh as well. While Ian turns to face Kenzie, as he looks up at her, he freezes.

"What's wrong, Ian?" Kenzie asks.

Ian does not answer right away, but is staring at himself in a mirror in the bedding department of the store. Ian is not really seeing his own reflection though. He is seeing Kayla.

"It's Kayla." Ian says softly out loud. "She is there, in the mirror, I can see her. She is lying down on a bed sleeping."

Jax and Kenzie run over to Ian to look and see if they can see what he is seeing as well. Unfortunately, they are only able to see the three of them looking back at themselves in the mirror.

"I don't get it. When Ian pulled Connor through the bathroom mirror on the train, I could see what he was seeing. But I don't see anything now but us," Kenzie expresses to Jax.

"Ian, are you sure you are seeing her?" Jax asks.

"Yes, it's her. I can't tell where she is, but I can tell she is in this timeline. That much I know for a fact," Ian replies back with excitement.

"How do you know she is in this timeline if you don't know where she is?" Jax questions Ian.

"Because I have only been able to use the mirror to see and move through present time. Kenzie lead me to Connor the first time I used a mirror to bring someone through it. The first time I actually saw Kenzie sleeping on a couch at her house was because I felt her needing me, like I can feel Kayla needing me now. This is how I know it is present time. Kayla needs me, but for some reason she can't connect with me telepathically," Ian concludes.

"Well, that does sound logical, and your powers could be evolving. The reason I say this is because Kenzie is unable to see what you see this time, but she did when you saved Connor," Jax implies.

"The difference then was that it was actually Kenzie that was leading me to her brother. She was describing his room and even Connor to me. This could be why she was able to see everything, to make sure I was in the right spot," Ian replies with his own conclusion of the previous events.

"Well, there is one way to find out," Kenzie mentions. "Why don't you try and reach into the mirror, like you did when you saw me. Remember, you knocked over the picture frame that woke me up."

Without any more words, Ian walks closer to the mirror and stretches out his arms towards the reflection. To his surprise, once his hands reach the mirror, they hit the class and almost knock it over. Luckily, Jax and Kenzie have quick reflexes and catch the mirror before it falls to the ground.

It was enough noise to catch the attention of the other customers and store employees. To keep from drawing any more attention to themselves, they decide not to purchase the bedding set Jax has taken so long to pick out, and just make their way to the store exit.

"I think we should head back to school now," Jax insists to the other two.

"I agree with you for once," Ian replies.

"But don't think you are getting off the hook on getting a new bedding set. Once we deal with this situation, we will come back for the set you picked out," Kenzie tells Jax.

***

Kayla wakes from her sleep with a startling feeling like she is being watched. She sits up in bed and starts looking around. At first glance, she does not find anything out of the ordinary. Then as she glances back past her bedroom mirror for a second time, she swears she can see the inside of a store in the mirror, instead of her own reflection. It only lasts for a second, then she sees herself reflecting back.

"What in the world was that?" she questions out loud. "Maybe I'm still dreaming."

Kayla, unable to shake the feeling of being watched, makes her way out of bed and over to the bedroom door. She unlocks the door and opens it enough to see the guard standing in his place right outside.

"Is there something I can help you with, ma'am?" the guard asks as Kayla just stares at him.

"No, thank you. Has anyone, or Mason, been here to see me in the last thirty minutes?" she asks the guard.

"No, ma'am. Why do you ask?" replies the guard.

"Do I need a reason to ask questions now?" Kayla barks back at the guard while shutting her bedroom door as quickly as possible. "Man, these guards sure are nosy."

Kayla begins her way back over to her bed, but before she makes it to her destination, she stops. She decides that she wants to check out the mirror on her dresser a little more.

"What can it hurt to just look and see if there is a camera in the mirror?" Kayla asks herself out loud. "There is no telling just how far Mason will go to keep an eye on me," she finishes as she reaches her dresser.

Now that she is standing directly in front of her dresser with a mirror on it, she begins to take a closer look at the mirror. She begins to run her hands along the sides, then the top and bottom of it, until she is satisfied that she feels that there are no wires connecting to it. *Doesn't mean he's not using wireless cameras,* she thinks to herself.

"There has to be some sort of camera here and I'm just overlooking it," Kayla said out loud. "He has to have hidden it really well, because I can't find it anywhere."

About that time, Kayla takes a quick nudge at the mirror. She does not know what to expect, but what happens next is not it.

As the mirror begins to steady from its rocking on the dresser, from her quick nudge, there is a clear vision of the same store Kayla thought she saw before in its reflection. Kayla stands back, just a little from the dresser, so she can take in what she is actually seeing.

"How is this even possible?" Kayla asks out loud. "This can't be a camera and I know this is not a television, so what in the world could this be?"

Just as she finishes her last sentence, the image flickers and disappears from the mirror. Kayla shakes the mirror again with the hopes of bringing back the image from before, but with no luck. After trying for about ten minutes, Kayla gives up for the night with frustration and decides to just go to bed. She turns and walks back over to her bed, climbs up into the soft and cozy covers, and falls back asleep.

Chapter 6

Let Brayden In?

Once Jax, Ian, and Kenzie make it back to the school, their mission is to head straight to the elevators. On the ride back from the Bed Bath & Beyond, which is a fifteen-minute drive from its Kirby Drive location in Houston, to the school downtown, they agreed that it is time they try Kenzie's suggestion of accessing the Time Keeper. They also agree that the safest place to try this experiment will be in Jax's room, since he does not have to share it with anyone, being he's a teacher and all.

They are still not sure if Ian will be able to access the Time Keeper, or what good it will do to help find Kayla if he can, but *desperate times call for desperate measures*. At least that is what Jax keeps telling himself to justify not telling the Council, or Maria, about what they are doing.

As the three of them enter the lobby of the school, they make a beeline to the elevators with hopes of not being stopped and questioned by anyone. They make it to the elevators without detection, but once the doors open, Brayden is standing there and decides to start asking questions.

This is the first time Brayden has even seen Ian since he refused to dream walk him, to bring him back from the memory he was stuck in for two days, and Kenzie had to do it.

"Where have you been? Ian, I have not seen you in a week! Are you okay? Are you mad at me or something?" Brayden starts with his questions.

"No, I'm not mad at you, or anyone actually. I have been just hanging out in the library a lot. I have not been trying to avoid you or anything," Ian lies to Brayden. "I'm sorry if I made you feel that way. I hate to cut this short, but we do have someplace we need to be right now. Can we catch up later?" Ian requests of Brayden, as he, Jax, and Kenzie all enter the elevator.

"Sure, but where are you headed to now? Can I come? I have finished all of my classes for the day, and I don't have anything else to do," Brayden asks with more of a begging tone than just asking.

Ian, I think it's time you let Brayden in on what's going on. He may be useful in case my power is not enough to bring you back, if needed, Kenzie thinks to Ian with her mind.

Ian gives Kenzie a nod of agreement and without saying anything to Jax, tells Brayden he can come with them.

"Yes Brayden, you can come with us. We may need your assistance with something, if you are not busy," Ian confirms to Brayden.

"I can?" Brayden replies.

"He can?" Jax asks Ian.

"Kenzie will explain to you now, if you give her permission to do so. Right, Kenzie?"

"Yes, but only if he says I can," she replies to Ian while looking directly at Jax. "So, do I have your permission?"

"Yes, you have my permission."

While the elevator doors close and Ian hits the button for Jax's floor, Kenzie is already in Jax's mind explaining what is going on and why she thinks they need Brayden. Once she finishes filling Jax in, he agrees with her, but wants to keep his involvement limited. Not only for his sake, but also for theirs. She agrees and will relay the information to Ian.

As the elevator makes its way closer to Jax's floor, Brayden is still talking. He has been talking non-stop since they all stepped onto the elevator. He is not talking about anything in particular, he is just talking about everything. He is talking about his lessons, teachers, and other students. Ian has not heard much of what Brayden has been saying, until he hears 'Maria' come up.

"Wait a minute, Brayden. Go back to the part about Maria again. I don't think I caught all of that," Ian asks of Brayden.

"You mean the part about how Maria left the school two days ago?" Brayden asks for confirmation.

"Yes, that part. Why did she leave, and where did she go?" Ian asks back to Brayden.

"No one knows, really. Two days ago, she just grabbed some of her things and left the school in a hurry. If there is a reason she left, they have not told the students. Jax, don't you know why Maria left?" Brayden inquires.

"No, this is the first I'm hearing about it. I have sort of been out of the teachers' loop for the past few days now. But this is something I will be looking into. Thank you for letting us know," Jax tells Brayden.

"No problem."

Ian looks over at Kenzie, but no words are exchanged between the two of them, verbally or telepathically. They both seem to be on the same page, wondering if Jax is telling the truth or not. They both think it's odd that the Head of the Believers can just up and leave and Jax not be informed about it. Kenzie gives Ian a nod, as if she already knows what Ian is planning for later. Right now, they have other pressing matters to attend to like trying to access the Time Keeper.

The elevator stops on Jax's floor, and once the doors open, he takes the lead to escort them to his room. His room is right next to the elevators, so their walk is very short. Jax slides in his key, gives it a turn, then opens the door for the other three to enter. Upon entering Jax's room, it is not quite as Ian, Brayden, and Kenzie have been expecting, not for a teacher anyway.

Jax's room is nothing more than a small studio apartment. He has a full kitchen along one wall, a table to eat at, a bed, and even a small sitting area. There are no walls to separate the areas. The only room that does have walls and a door is the bathroom. His wall facing the outside is nothing more than floor-to-ceiling windows, which brings back the memories Junior had shown Ian of Jax in a red bow tie at a party in a penthouse rooftop room with floor-to-ceiling windows all around it in New York City. Ian knows he is not here for a party though.

Now that everyone is in Jax's room, he shuts his bedroom door and locks it. He instructs the others to take a seat anywhere for the time being. Jax needs to make a few preparations for what they are about to attempt, just in case it works, or goes horribly wrong.

While the others are taking their seats, they can't help but notice the view through the wall of windows.

"Wow Jax! You have an awesome view of the city from your room. What is that building over there?" Ian asks Jax, while pointing towards one of the floor-to-ceiling windows along the wall.

"Oh, that is the Toyota Center. It is an indoor arena, mostly used by the Houston Rockets basketball team, to play their games in. It is also used, however, for the occasional concert when the Houston Rockets are not playing." Jax explains to all three of them. "Now, let's get back to business."

Jax is going to use his bed for Ian to lie down on while he is attempting to access the Time Keeper. There is enough space on both sides of the bed where Brayden can stand on one side, while Jax and Kenzie can stand on the other. Brayden and Kenzie are both prepared to enter Ian's mind if needed, in an emergency situation only. While Jax prepares, Brayden steps to the side with Ian.

"Ian, I have to ask you something, and it's very important," Brayden tells Ian.

"Okay, what is it?"

"Before I ask, let me start by telling you that I'm sorry I would not dream walk you when you were stuck for those two days last time. I refused to dream walk you, because I made you a promise. I told you I would never dream walk you again without your permission first, so that leads me to ask. Do I have your permission to dream walk you this time if Jax feels it's an emergency?" Brayden expresses to Ian.

"First, you don't have to apologize to me for not dream walking me. I have had an idea why you didn't, and I totally respect you honoring my wishes. That is what a true friend does, honor a friend's request even if others try to make you betray them by telling you it's the right thing to do. Now, yes, I give you permission to dream walk me, but you don't have to just because Jax tells you to. I want you to use your best judgement, along with Kenzie's, and help decide if I need help. I trust you both, so if you need Kenzie's advice on anything, just think her name loudly in your head, and she will answer your thoughts. This way Jax is out of the loop, for now. Are you okay with that?" Ian open-heartedly replies back to Brayden.

"Yes, I like that idea even better," Brayden replies.

The two of them share a quick hand shake and return to the other two in the room. It's not like they were very far from them in Jax's studio apartment.

Once they are back to make a group of four, Jax instructs Ian to take his place on the bed, Brayden to take one side of the bed and Kenzie to stand next to him on the other side.

"Okay Ian, once you are comfortable and willing to give this a try, I want you to try and access something that you have stored in the Time Keeper, if you have been able to do so. I think the easiest approach would be to access your own memories before trying to access one of your relatives' memories," Jax clarifies to the group.

"That actually sounds like a great way to start," Ian agrees with Jax.

Ian lays back on the bed with a quick thought to Kenzie, *I bet the other bed set would be more comfortable than this one. Too bad we left the store before he could get it!*

Kenzie gives out a short, but very loud laugh at the thought. Then she looks over at Jax, and the look on his face reminds her that this is not the time for fun and games. Even though Ian is the one joking, she is the one caught laughing.

"Sorry, Jax. I was thinking of something I shouldn't have been. I'm ready now," Kenzie apologizes to Jax.

"Are we all ready to try this now? Does anyone else have something funny they would like to think of, or share with the rest of us? If not, then let's give this a go please," Jax asks of the group.

No one says a word, nor a thought, to each other. They can tell Jax is very serious.

Ian has taken off the Time Keeper from his wrist and is holding it tightly in his hands. He is now thinking of the only memory he can recall that he stored in the Time Keeper. The memory of his telling Maria about Kayla. That is at least the first memory he actually has tried to store in the Time Keeper.

Ian can recall only one memory that he has tried to store in the Time Keeper, and that moment is when he met Maria. He thinks of that moment of seeing her in the Sky Lounge with the rest of the group. He is also thinking about how Maria made him feel with her smug attitude about what he knew and didn't know about the Council. Then he thinks of how she threw Kayla's name around like it was nothing, like SHE was nothing. The more he thinks about this moment, the more he feels how telling Maria may have been a mistake, and this infuriates him even more. But for some reason, nothing seems to be working.

"Is it working?" Jax asks.

"Not that I am aware of. I don't know how to make it work. Remember, the only times I've seen memories are when Junior lead me to them. But of course that was only speeding up time to make me eighteen, so I could access the Time Keeper. I've never done this on my own before, and it's not like there are instructions," Ian snaps back to Jax. "I think I am missing something."

"Are you trying the filing system we figured out? The one with making something in that memory red, so you can focus on it?"

"Yes, I tried that, but I still think we are missing something."

"What?" Jax asks Ian.

"If I knew what it was, then it wouldn't be missing now, would it?"

It is at this moment when Ian thinks of Kayla's ring. "It may be the ring Kayla gave me, or gives me when I turn eighteen, and the Time

Keeper together that I need to access it. I remember I was not wearing them when I passed out from my shower, or when Kenzie brought me back from that memory I was stuck in, but I was wearing them both when I was in the memory."

"But the ring's power should not still be attached to it. Once it was used to wipe Kayla from history, that's all the power it had. Its purpose was completed, so its power should also be gone."

"All I can tell you is that I had them both on in the memory, so there is something to the ring still. We need that ring Jax."

"Perfect. Where is the ring now?" Jax ask Ian.

"I'm not sure. I have not seen it since the memory. I took it off to take a shower, set it on my dresser with the Time Keeper, then when I came out of the shower, I noticed the Time Keeper missing from my dresser. Before I could look for it, I passed out and was stuck in the memory and was wearing them both. After Kenzie woke me up, and I went back to my room, only the Time Keeper was on my dresser. I have been so caught up with finding out about Sebastian's half-sister, I didn't bother looking for the ring," Ian finishes.

"Well, I say we start looking for the ring in our room then. It has to be in there, it would not just walk out of our room on its own. Maybe it fell behind your dresser," Brayden says to Ian.

"Only one way to find out. Let's go to our room and begin looking behind and under everything in our room. We will leave no stone unturned, so to speak," Ian instructs the others, and off they go.

Chapter 7

Maria?

"Search this entire room. First, can someone help me move this dresser so I can look behind it," Ian instructs the others, and asks for help at the same time, as they start the search for the missing ring Kayla had given him. "It has to be in this room somewhere."

Brayden begins walking over to the dresser to help Ian move it, when all of a sudden, the dresser moves forward, on its own, or so they think. Both Ian and Brayden look at each other, thinking the other had something to do with the dresser moving.

"How did you do that?" Ian asks Brayden.

"I was about to ask you the same thing," Brayden replies back to Ian.

"If I had the power to move the dresser like that, then why would I ask for help in the first place?" Ian replies to Brayden.

"I don't know. Maybe you have a new power now, and you are just showing it off?" Brayden snaps back to Ian.

"I'm sorry," comes a small whisper from behind Kenzie. "I just wanted to help."

"Connor? You moved that dresser?" Kenzie turns around and asks Connor with a look of shock on her face.

"Kenzie, wait. Connor, it's okay if you moved the dresser. No one is mad or upset with you. I think Kenzie is just a little surprised. I guess this is something you never told her?" Jax is speaking softly to Connor. He wants to keep him relaxed.

Connor's classes had finished for the day by the time they were heading up to Ian and Brayden's room, so instead of leaving him alone in his room, they all decided to bring him along. They are sure they made the right decision now, with him having powers and all.

"No. I never told anyone, not even Kenzie. I was afraid that our parents would treat me like they were treating Kenzie if they found out, so I never said anything. Plus, I was afraid they would tell Mr. Mason. I thought that since we are safe at this school, I could help you and use my powers. I'm sorry," Connor repeats again, this time looking directly at Kenzie.

Kenzie bends down and grabs Connor with a tight hug. She whispers in his ear, "You have nothing to be sorry for. You are now able to be free and be who you are meant to be. You, I mean we are safe here at this school," Kenzie finishes and releases him from her grasp.

"Well, thank you, Connor, for moving the dresser for me. By the way, awesome power," Ian says to Connor with a smile. "Now we can all get back to searching for the ring. And if you need anything heavy moved, Connor is your man," Ian replies to the group while looking at Connor and giving him a wink of approval.

They all can tell by the look on Connor's face that Ian's words mean the world to him. He has a look of pure encouragement and acceptance across his face.

Now that Connor has come out about having powers, everyone is back to searching the room. Ian looks behind the dresser Connor moved for him, but no sign of the ring. "Connor, do you mind giving the dresser a little push back to where it goes? The ring is not behind it," Ian asks Connor for his assistance.

"You got it, Ian!" Connor replies with enthusiasm and confidence. Then with a little mental nudge, he pushes the dresser back against the wall. With all of the excitement that has just gone on with everyone now knowing about his powers, he may have given the dresser a little bit too much of a nudge. That extra boost sends the dresser back hitting the wall pretty hard, but it didn't cause any damage.

"Thank you, Connor," Ian relays to him showing no sign of being upset with him, which keeps Connor at ease.

"How is everyone else doing? Any sign of the ring, yet?" Ian asks the group.

"Nothing from this side of the room," replies Brayden.

"Nothing from over here either, Ian," replies Jax from the bathroom.

"We got nothing either," Kenzie sounds off for Connor and herself. Connor is lowering the small table, which Ian and Brayden share, back to the ground.

"Great job on the table, Connor," Ian commends him. "Okay, if the ring is not here, then someone has to have taken it. I set the Time Keeper and the ring both right here on the top of this dresser before I took a shower. Upon returning from the shower, and before I passed out, I noticed the Time Keeper was missing. But while I was stuck in the memory of Sebastian and his father, which I'll explain later, I was wearing them both. Then when I got back to our room, once Kenzie brought me out of that memory, the ring was the only thing missing. I didn't think much about it at the time," Ian explains to everyone.

"Who could have taken it, and why?" Jax asks the question this time.

"Jax, I know you may not want to hear this, but the only person I can think of is Maria. She did not believe my story about Kayla, and then she just up and leaves the school. With her abrupt departure from the school and the ring missing, it does not seem like a coincidence to me," Ian tells Jax.

"Maria is Head of the Believers. Why would she take the ring Kayla gave you and leave the school? What would she, or Believers, have to gain from any of this?" Jax asks back to the group, not just to Ian. "If there is anything between the

Believers and that ring, I would know about it, or they would have taken it weeks ago."

"How long have you really known Maria? Personally, I mean?" Brayden asks this time.

"I have spoken to her for many years, and her reputation precedes her. But to be honest, this is the first time I have met her face to face. But what does that have to do with what type of person she is? I trust her completely, based on the years of conversations and information she has given me," Jax defends Maria.

"No one is saying she has not been honest with you over the years, but again time has been changed. When Kayla erased herself from this timeline, who knows what other ramifications it had? I don't doubt that you feel Maria is good inside, but we have to consider everything right now. She is the only one that truly stands out as having suspicious behavior, correct?" Ian calmly asks Jax.

"Maybe if we can set history back on the right path, with Kayla in it, then maybe the Maria you know will be the same one as before."

"Before I go and start accusing anyone of anything, I am going to go down to the headmaster's office and see if I can find out why Maria left. As far as we know, she may have had to leave for Believer business. So, before I let anyone go dragging her name through the mud, I want to get all the facts first. Do you mind keeping your opinions and assumptions to yourselves about Maria until I come back with more details from the headmaster?" Jax requests of the group.

"Yes, Jax, of course. We do not want to ruin anyone's name, or honor, with misguided assumptions or false information. The more we know the better," Ian assures Jax of their compliance.

"Thank you all. I will be back in a little bit. I'm going to head down to see what I can find out from the headmaster himself," Jax concludes as he is walking towards Ian's bedroom door, opens it and exits, shutting the door behind him.

***

"I think this might be something you may want. Somehow Ian claims that Kayla gave, or gives, this ring to him on his eighteenth birthday. I'm not sure how either of those can, or have, happened yet, but here's the ring," Maria tells Mason while handing him the ring she has taken from Ian's dresser. She took it the day Ian woke up in the infirmary, which was a week ago, but she has just now been able to take leave from school without anyone noticing.

"Nothing is impossible. You of all people should know this, Maria."

"I will say there is something special about this ring and his watch, because neither of them were present in his room until he woke up that is. That is when they both appeared out of the blue on his dresser."

"Now I know I nothing is impossible, but what in the world are you talking about? How can something just appear out of thin air? And how can she give him a ring for a birthday he has not even had yet? Better than that, how can she give him anything considering, from what I understand, she doesn't even exist in this timeline now? You are beginning to sound like a crazy person," Mason says to Maria with skepticism.

"I am just telling you what I saw with my own two eyes, and what I found out. Do what you want with the information and the ring, but I'm risking everything by working with you. Ian already does not trust me, because I lied to him about not knowing about Kayla. He knows that the Council is aware of everything, so for me to tell him I know nothing about Kayla raises suspicion and distrust for me. And, while we are on the subject of distrust, why didn't you inform me about Kenzie and her brother Connor?" Maria questions Mason.

"Who do you think you are, questioning me? Kenzie is none of your concern, nor the Council's. I had a special arrangement with Jerry and Delores for Kenzie's well-being, and her 'brother' Connor is nothing special like she is. He just happened to be a bonus for the Greens for their help, but that does not matter now. Since they failed to keep Kenzie away from all of you, the Council, the school, and Ian, I have sent them back to their timeline. They are now nothing more than history from the sixties," Mason explains.

"Now, you also need to remember that I am the only reason you are Head of the Believers right now, so MIND YOUR PLACE WITH ME! Is that understood?" Mason reminds Maria very loudly.

"Understood, Mason," his name spits out of Maria's mouth. "But do you need to be reminded of what seat I hold? With or without your help, I AM Head of the Believers, and if you try and hide anything else from me, you just may see what I can do from my seat as Head Believer," Maria threatens Mason.

The two of them stand and stare at each other, knowing each of them means business, and then calmly relax, dropping their shoulders a bit and give each other a small smile.

"Now that we have reached a mutual understanding on just what and how much damage we can cause each other, let's get back to business," Maria suggests to Mason.

"That sounds like a splendid idea. Why don't we just take the ring to Kayla and see if we can get some kind of reaction from her, by showing her the ring? That should tell us whether or not what you have heard is the truth," Mason suggests.

"Now, that has to be the smartest thing you have said since I have arrived today. Why don't you lead the way to Kayla?" Maria smirks.

"Right this way, please," Mason tells Maria while opening his arms and stretching out his right arm, as if to say, 'Ladies first.'

Maria, of course, does not fall for such foolishness and just stands there giving Mason a 'nice try' look and says, "Well, get to leading the way."

***

"Well, now that Jax left I might as well fill the two of you in on what happened to me, while I was stuck in that memory for those two days.

I realize now that the reason I noticed the Time Keeper missing from my dresser, as I was passing out, was because I was wearing it while I was stuck in the memory. Not only was I wearing the Time Keeper, but I was also wearing the ring Kayla had given me. I just didn't notice the ring because it is smaller and not that noticeable. But when I woke up in the memory I had them both on.

The memory I was stuck in for two days was of Sebastian and his father, Jacob Helen. I was not sure of his father's name until Kenzie was pulled into a daydream, or memory, I had while I was waiting on the elevator in the library the day I became stuck in the other memory for two days. She actually got on the elevator as I was going to my room to take a shower and a nap, then she told me his name. Somehow the ring and watch wanted me to see that memory, because I was wearing them both then as well. Those two together are very powerful, or they would not have been able to pull Kenzie into a memory they were giving me, so she could find out Sebastian's father's name. I was not even wearing them when I passed out. I took them off to take my shower. The next thing I know is that I'm stuck in a memory, and they put themselves on me. That is why I have not said anything about what happened to me, and I made Kenzie promise not to tell either.

If not for Kenzie, I would not know Sebastian's father's name, or where to look for his other child. Now that you both know, Connor and Brayden, please don't tell anyone else. But now you can see why we need to find the ring," Ian finishes telling the story of how Kenzie figured out Jacob Helen's name and about being stuck in a memory for two days. He felt better now that the rest of the group knew.

Chapter 8

The Ring?

"I have an idea," Kenzie says to the remaining members of the group once Ian finishes filling in the remaining group in on what he actually saw while stuck in Jacob Helen's memory for two days.

"What do you have on your mind, Kenzie? I can already tell by the crooked smile on your face, it may not be something that Jax would approve of," Ian urges Kenzie to continue.

"Well, I'm sure he would approve of it, but only after hours of explaining how we are going to be safe, and follow his lead, and all the other things he would need to hear. But he's not here, so this is what I am thinking," Kenzie prepares the group, which now consists of Connor, Brayden, Ian and herself.

"Go on! Don't just leave us hanging here," Brayden says with excitement.

"Ian, you know that Brayden can dream walk, and I can pop in and out of your mind at any time, right?" Kenzie starts off with her idea.

"Yes, but I don't see where this is going, yet," Ian answers her question.

"I am thinking that maybe we try something a little different this time. Since we don't have the ring to use with the Time Keeper, why don't we try using Brayden's power and my power together, along with the Time Keeper? We just might be able to get you access to the Time Keeper that way," Kenzie explains.

"Okay, I'm starting to see what you mean," Ian says out loud.

"I don't," Brayden says, while looking at Connor, hoping he is not the only one that does not understand. Unfortunately, he is the only one that is not understanding, Connor knows exactly what they are talking about.

"Brayden, just listen. We let Ian go to sleep while he is wearing the Time Keeper. Once he is asleep, you and I both will go into his mind at the same time. Since he will only be dreaming, I can tell him what he should be dreaming about. It will be like the time when I had to describe Connor and even his room to Ian, so he could pull him through the mirror on the train. This will give you the ability to help him towards the dream I am suggesting. Hopefully, something I describe to Ian will be a trigger to unlock the Time Keeper and let a memory out. Once the memory is out, you will be able to guide Ian to the memory instead of his dream. Then we can both stay with him, in case he needs us to bring him back," Kenzie finishes her plan in detail. "At least I hope that is something you can do when you are dream walking someone. You can do this, right?"

"And what grade are you in again?" Brayden asks Kenzie with a smile. "That plan does not sound like one from a typical fifth grader. And I have been able to make contact with people in their dreams before, but I have not really tried to make someone leave one dream for another. But I will do what I can."

"Let's just say that Cooper has the best schools in the state of Texas. We may be a bit more advanced than other schools in Texas, being a small town and small schools, it's more like a private school, but public. Just because Cooper is a small country town does not mean we do not get an exceptional education," Kenzie replies with Bulldawg Pride.

"I will agree with you there, Kenzie. I like this idea too, but do you think we have enough time for me to fall asleep and you two to do everything you need to before Jax returns?" Ian asks.

"I guess we will find out. Now, why don't you go and lie down on your bed and relax so you can try and fall asleep. While you do that, I will communicate with Brayden and Connor in their thoughts, so we don't interrupt you. We will prepare the room to be a bit darker, and of course we will lock the door," Kenzie has taken the lead on this mission. "Now go get comfortable, Ian. We got this!"

Brayden, we need to be prepared for whatever we may come up against in Ian's mind. I am only used to dealing with thoughts and memories, not dreams, so I will be counting on your expertise with getting Ian from one dream to another. Is there anything you can tell me that I should be aware of? Kenzie thinks to Connor and Brayden as not to disturb Ian falling asleep.

"Well there is ..." Brayden is cut off quickly.

Think your words, don't talk out loud. Remember we are thinking conversations so we don't disturb Ian's sleeping? Kenzie cuts Brayden off.

Sorry, this is all new to me. I am not used to thinking my thoughts to people. Half the time when I talk to people they don't listen. Anyway, back on topic. I'm not sure what I can tell you to expect, because I don't know what is different from dream and a memory. To me, dream walking is pretty easy, but I also have never tried to move anyone from one dream to another. So I guess we will both find out if it's possible. Brayden thinks back to the other two, Connor and Kenzie, not understanding that Kenzie is the only one who can hear his thoughts.

What do I do? Am I supposed to just sit here and wait for you both to finish? Connor asks.

Connor, you have the most important job. You are to watch over all of us and make sure we are all okay. You are going to be our protector. Are you okay with that job? I know it's a big job, but I have all the faith in the world that you can do it, Kenzie sounds off to her little brother, with a connection with Brayden so he can hear.

Yes, I can do it. I will make sure you are all safe. Nothing will hurt you while I'm on watch.

Good to know. Now let's finish getting the room ready and get ready ourselves for this experiment, Kenzie finishes with the group's instructions.

Why can't I hear Connor? All I hear is you?

Because I can link you both together to hear me, but you can't hear or speak to each other. My gift does not work that way, but relax, we are all on the same page, Kenzie explains to Brayden.

***

"Here we are. This is Kayla's room. Would you like to do the honors of knocking on her door, or would you like to just barge in?" Mason asks Maria, while looking at the guard standing beside the door. Both Mason and the guard know how serious Kayla is about her private time, so they know knocking will be best.

"I'm sure the guard can announce our presence," Maria states while looking at the guard. "Can you do that simple task for us?"

The guard and Mason both were secretly hoping she would have wanted to barge in on Kayla herself, so they could watch what came with that type of interruption in Kayla's free time. With the disappointment of Maria not barging in, the guard turns to Maria and answers, "Yes, ma'am."

The guard gives Kayla's bedroom door three soft knocks while calling out her name, "Kayla, are you busy? You have two visitors."

"Yes, I am extremely busy being locked in my room like a prisoner. So, could you ask them to return when I am released? That would be great," Kayla yells back to the guard.

"I'm sorry, Kayla, but that is not possible."

"And why not?"

"Mason is here with a guest. I suggest you open your door, please," the guard explains to Kayla.

"Well, why didn't you just say so? I wish someone would have told me the prisoner was part of his tour of the building for new recruits, so I could have been more prepared. Since his guards are traitors and escaping, I sure wouldn't want to disrupt his hiring process. We all know he could use some better guards around here," Kayla sarcastically replies.

"She sure has a mouth on her. I don't know how you put up with it," Maria turns and tells Mason. "I'm glad I don't have to deal with her on a daily basis."

Just as Maria finishes what she has to say to Mason, Kayla's bedroom door flies open and she just stands there looking at the pair of them, Maria and Mason.

"What is it that I can do for the both of you at this moment? Or did you just come by to show off your prisoner?" Kayla speaks directly at Mason.

"Actually, Kayla, we do not want to take up too much of your time, as I can see you must be a busy woman. To be honest, we really just have one question for you, then we will be on our way. Is that okay with you?" Maria asks Kayla.

"Fine, but who are you anyway?" She replies.

"Who I am is no concern of yours. We just need you to answer one simple question for us. By the mouth you have on you, simple seems to be right up your alley," Maria tells Kayla with a stern look of authority.

"If you call me simple one more time, you may not be able to get the answer to your question, and it will not be because I won't give it to you. You just won't be able to hear it. Do you get my drift?" Kayla snaps back to Maria.

Maria does not answer after that statement from Kayla.

"Enough, Kayla! Now do you mind holding out your hand, palm up and open please?" Mason instructs her.

Kayla turns her stare away from Maria and does as Mason has asked of her. As she is standing there, Mason sets a small silver ring in her open palm.

Kayla looks down at the ring, then looks up to Mason. She has a look of shock on her face.

I knew it! Maria thinks to herself. *I knew this ring has something to do with the two of them. Ian is telling the truth about Kayla giving him this ring!*

"The answer to your simple question is NO! NO, I will not marry you! What in the world would make you think I would ever marry you? You are the worst person I have ever met, and you bring this woman with you, as what? A witness? Why ..."

"STOP!" Mason shouts at Kayla. "I am not asking you to marry me. Why in the world would you think I would?"

"Why else does a man gives a woman a ring? I am too young for you anyway," Kayla flips her open hand over, the one holding the small silver ring Mason has placed in it, letting it fall down to the floor, as part of her reply to Mason's question.

"I am not trying to give you an engagement ring. I want you to look at this ring closely, and tell me if you recognize it," Mason states as he bends down to pick up the ring, before it can roll off down the hallway, and places it back in Kayla's hand.

"No, I don't recognize it. Why would I? Is this not the first time you have proposed to me? Do you keep doing this to me and then erase my memory somehow, in hopes that I will say yes one day? You are a sick man, a very sick man, Mason. You are even sicker than I thought after you made me a prisoner. And lady, you must be just as sick as he is to keep watching him get turned down over and over again. If you don't mind, take this ring back and do not try this again," Kayla rambles on and on as she gives Mason the ring back and slams her door.

Once her door is shut, she ran over to her bed and lays back down, this time covering her head with her pillow, thinking, *How did they get Ian's ring, and why did I just say all of that stuff?*

Man, I was way off, Maria thinks to herself with a chuckle.

"Is that the type of reaction you were looking for?" Maria asks Mason.

"Not even close," he replies back.

"She has no clue what this ring is, does she?" Maria asks Mason.

"I would say no. By the way guard, if you repeat a word of what just transpired here to anyone, I will make sure your life is horrible for the rest of your life. Understood?"

"Yes, sir," the guard replies to Mason, hiding a small smile inside, as he watches the pair walk back down the hall, back in the direction from where they came.

***

As Ian falls asleep, he is on his own bed, which is much easier to sleep on than on Jax's. He is not thinking of anything as he is dozing off. He wants to just sleep and dream. Dream like a normal seventeen-year-old boy dreams. Dream of a future career, or a made-up world, or just going on a vacation with his mom and dad, or a girl. Then the next thing he knows, he is dreaming.

He is dreaming of a trip that John and Donna, his parents had taken him on when he was a bit younger. This was the first time he had ever been snow skiing, but this dream is different than the original memory. In this one he has an older brother, Pete, a little sister Ashley, and a little brother John Dock. He knows Pete must be the oldest because he has a daughter with him, Ian's niece, Kourtney. Oh what fun they are all having, until Kenzie joins in.

"Are you ready to begin, Ian?" Kenzie asks while trying to get his attention. "Brayden, I need you to pull Ian outside of this cabin. Can you do that?"

"I think so," Brayden tells Kenzie. Brayden is there in Ian's dream standing next to him.

Brayden reaches out and slowly takes Ian by his left arm, and Ian begins to slowly shake his head. It's like he is coming to from being asleep, while still asleep.

"It's okay Ian. It's me, Brayden, and Kenzie is here too. Remember, we are here with you? We are here to help you unlock the Time Keeper," Brayden pleads with Ian as he can feel his resistance as he is being pulled from his dream.

"Kenzie, do something. This is not working. This dream has some hold on him, and I can't pull him away. I'm not even sure I will ever be able to," Brayden begs for help.

"Ian! Ian! Can you hear me? It's me, Kenzie. We are here to help you. Can't you see me? I am right in front of you," Kenzie is shouting at Ian with desperation, but she is getting no response.

"Kenzie, what do we do?" Brayden asks with panic in his voice.

"I don't know exactly. I didn't think dreams could hold this much power over a person's mind. It's like dreams are what keeps a person going on with their lives, so by trying to take a person away from their dreams, it is like trying to take a part of them away from themselves. Someone's thoughts are so much different than their dreams," Kenzie tells Brayden. "Pull harder!"

Stop! I got it from here. Thank you both for trying to help, are thoughts Kenzie and Brayden hear inside Ian's mind, catching them both by utter surprise. Those words are the last they hear before both of them are pushed out by someone, or something, very powerful.

"Who, or what, was that?" Brayden is asking Kenzie out loud, as they are both sitting beside Ian's bed in his bedroom. Both of them having been kicked out of Ian's mind.

"What happened to you while you both were in Ian's mind? Why are you both out here now and not in there helping him?" Connor asks them both.

"I don't know. But I think this is an emergency, don't you? We need to get Jax back here now," Kenzie tells Brayden while looking at Connor.

"What are you not telling me? I was supposed to be on the lookout to make sure you were all safe. What happened?" Connor insists.

"Connor, I will explain it all when Jax is here, but I just don't have time to explain it right now. It was not anything you did. You did exactly what you were supposed to do. This was something none of us could have ever foreseen," Kenzie explains in more detail to Connor. "Now, will you stay here and watch Ian while we go and get help?"

"Yes, anything for Ian," Connor replies as they quickly leave the room to go get Jax.

Chapter 9

The Fight?

"When are we actually going to go skiing?" Ian asks his father John Dock III.

"In just a little bit. Be patient Ian. We just got here. Go help your brothers unpack the car. The sooner it is unpacked, the sooner we can hit the slopes," John tells Ian.

Ian does as his father asks of him and runs outside to the car to help finish unpacking it with his two brothers, Pete and John Dock. Pete also has his daughter, Kortney, outside playing in the snow, while he helps unload the car. "Get over here and get all of these heavy suitcases Ian," Pete speaks loudly over to Ian.

"I'm on my way, but you know I can't carry all of those bags on my own. Why isn't Ashley helping? She's stronger than I am," Ian replies to Pete as he heads towards the car.

"Whatever you can't get I will get," John Dock tells Ian. "Just get what you can and I'll get the rest. Deal? And you know as well as we do, Ashley is not going to help."

"Deal!"

As Ian takes a moment to enjoy this feeling of togetherness, Pete ruins the moment by dropping two large bags at his feet. Ian takes the hint and picks up the heavy bags.

Ian is so excited! This is his first-time skiing and the first vacation he can remember taking with his mom and dad. The difference from this dream and his original memory of this event, is that he has siblings in this dream, and even has a niece. He is drawn to the overwhelming feeling of a bigger family.

Being an only child, Ian has only felt one type of love, which changed the day he met Kayla. The closer he and Kayla became, the more he felt love for her as a sister. The more his thoughts of Kayla take over this dream, the more things start to change. Ian notices that the family he is dreaming of starts to vanish, and the cabin and snow are also gone now. Everything has turned into a big white room, one he has only seen once before.

"What is going on here?" Ian asks, not only in his dream, but out loud while he is still asleep where Connor can hear him.

"Ian, can you hear me? It's Connor. Brayden and Kenzie went to get help, or Jax, I think."

Ian does not answer Connor, but also receives no response in his dream. Confused, Ian calls out loud for Brayden and Kenzie. Again, no reply.

"Who is this controlling my thoughts?" Ian asks in his dream and in his sleep again.

"Ian, what is going on? You are scaring me, and I don't know what to do," Connor pleads with Ian.

Ian again does not reply to Connor and again receives no answer from inside his dream.

Connor, now scared, thinks as hard as he can to Kenzie. He remembers her saying that she does not have to be near someone to hear their thoughts, so he wants to see if she can hear him.

Kenzie, if you can hear me, I need you here with me now. I'm scared and don't know what to do. Ian is talking again in his sleep, but not to me. I don't know what to do. Please help, Connor thinks as hard as he can to Kenzie.

***

Kenzie and Brayden are in the headmaster's waiting room waiting for Jax to finish talking with him. Jax is trying to see if the headmaster knows where Maria may have gone, or for what reason. He also wants to know if it was for official Believer, or Council, business, why he was not asked to join. Jax has been in the headmaster's office for over thirty minutes now.

"What is taking them so long?" Brayden asks Kenzie, with a hint of her using her gift to find out.

"I don't know. But I tell you one thing, I will not barge into Jax's mind again, not without his permission to find out. Just like you with Ian, I made a promise to Jax. So you can stop with the 'look' because it will not work."

"But this is an emergency!"

"Well, Jax and I did not stipulate if emergencies would be allowed, so we will wait until they are finished talking, and Jax comes out," Kenzie ends that line of the conversation.

As they are both sitting there in the headmaster's waiting room, Kenzie suddenly jerks straight up in her chair. She looks like she just got a shock from the chair she was sitting in.

"What's wrong?" Brayden inquires. "Are you okay?"

"It's Ian. Connor is scared about something. He is thinking of me and wants me to come back, or both of us to come back. I'm not sure what is happening, but I think it has something to do with Ian's dream," Kenzie explains.

"How does Connor know that?" Brayden replies. "He can't dream walk too, can he?"

"No, don't be silly, now is not the time. It has to do with something about Ian talking in his sleep. I have to go to Connor NOW. Wait here for Jax to finish, then the both of you hurry back to your room," Kenzie instructs Brayden. Then she is on her feet, out of the chair, and on her way out of the waiting room, rushing to help Connor.

I'm on my way to you, Connor. Hang in there. Are you going to be okay until I get there? Kenzie thinks to Connor.

WOW! How are you doing that from so far away? I thought my power was cool, Connor thinks back.

Connor, I know this is new to you, but we need to think about Ian right now, are her thoughts back to him.

Sorry, I think we will be okay until y'all get here, but then again, I really don't know what is going on. I just know what I am hearing does not sound good, Connor explains to Kenzie.

Well, right now it is just going to be you and me. Brayden is still waiting for Jax to finish with the headmaster, then they will be right back. I am almost there so hold tight, are her last thoughts to Connor as the elevator doors open.

***

Now that Connor's telepathic conversation with Kenzie has ended, he turns his attention back to Ian. Meanwhile, Ian is still asleep, tossing and turning, as if he is fighting some internal moral issues. As Connor is waiting on Kenzie to arrive, he notices Ian stops talking in his sleep, but he is still moving about on the bed. It's more like shaking than moving. Connor grabs one of Ian's quilts and throws it over him, just in case he is shaking because he is cold. About that time Kenzie comes rushing into the room.

"What's happening now?" she asks Connor.

"I don't know. He just started shaking, so I put that quilt over him in case he's cold," Connor tells Kenzie.

"That's a good idea Connor. He just maybe cold as he is going through whatever it is in his mind right now," Kenzie expresses to Connor.

Back in Ian's dream state, the white room has turned into an old pub. He can see poorly dressed men and women sitting at an old wooden tables with wood chairs. Some other people are standing at the bar. There are no modern items in the room, like a pool table, a stage for performers, or even an electronic cash register. Ian now knows he is in a memory, not a dream.

"Where am I, and how did I get here?" Ian asks, not realizing that what he is saying while asleep, he is also saying out loud, talking in his sleep. Both Connor and Kenzie can hear him.

This time, Connor, along with Kenzie, does not try to answer Ian, but merely start to listen to what he says. They, Kenzie most of all, are hoping to get some clues as to what is going on inside Ian's mind before Brayden and Jax returns.

Ian still receives no answer to his questions. Then two men, who are sitting at a table in the corner of the pub, start yelling at each other. From what Ian can gather from it, the yelling starts over a card game of some kind.

"You are cheating! You always cheat! That's how you always win," one of the men shouts loudly at the other.

"I ain't no cheat, Grayson. You should know that," the other man replies.

"You are a liar and a cheat, Sebastian. Not only do you cheat in cards, but also with other men's wives," Grayson yells back to Sebastian.

Sebastian and Grayson? Both of them standing right in front of me, Ian thinks to himself.

Before Ian knows what is really happening, Sebastian is taking a swing at Grayson, knocking him back away from the card table.

"Hey, you two! Knock it off, or take it outside," says the barkeep, Marty, while holding a shotgun in his hands.

"You got it, Marty. Come on, Sebastian, let's take this outside and finish it like men. Unless you are afraid or something," Grayson smirks at Sebastian.

Sebastian thinks little about this fight that is about to happen, as they have had many before. He knows he will just use the Time Keeper to store this moment and then go back and change the outcome later.

First, he will find out how Grayson found out about his indiscretions. Then he will make sure he does not find out about them the next time around. So, Sebastian willingly follows Grayson outside the pub.

Grayson is already waiting for Sebastian in the back alley as he comes walking out the back door. Suddenly Grayson catches Sebastian by surprise with a right hook.

Ian, somehow, went from inside the pub to the back alley in a flash, just in time to see the blow to Sebastian's face.

"Holy cow!" Ian shouts from the sidelines in the alley.

No one seems to be able to even notice Ian's presence. It is then obvious to Ian that he is only an observer in this memory. But his outburst catches the attention of Kenzie and Connor.

"Connor, I'm going to try and go back into Ian's mind to see what is happening. If anything goes wrong, I want you to run and get Jax and Brayden. Even if Jax is not through with his meeting with the headmaster, I want you to interrupt their meeting if you have too. Whatever you do, make sure you bring them both back here, fast. Do you understand?" Kenzie demands of Connor.

"Yes, but are you going to be okay?" Connor asks, worried about his sister even though she is older than he is. "I mean, do you think it's safe for you to go back in? The last time you and Brayden went in you both got kicked out."

"I will be fine, but do as I ask please," are her final instructions to Connor. "I just want to see what is going on in his mind right now, or find out who is controlling his memories if I can."

Kenzie shuts her eyes and concentrates on Ian. She thinks as hard as she can about the thoughts and words he said out loud. She is trying to enter Ian's thoughts, but she is being blocked somehow. Kenzie keeps trying, but still keeps getting pushed back.

Who are you, and why won't you let me in to talk to Ian? Kenzie speaks with her thoughts to whatever is keeping her out of Ian's mind. *Let me IN!*

NO. Please, let me do this. You and your friend will not be able to access the Time Keeper. I can and already have. Ian is safe with me, I swear, comes a voice only Kenzie can hear with her mind.

How can I trust you? You have kicked Brayden and me out of Ian's mind and we are here to help Ian. Where were you when he was stuck in a memory for two days last time? Kenzie thinks back to the voice.

It's hard to explain. I was there, but I was very weak. I only became stronger a few minutes ago, when my mother held a ring in the palm of her hand, replies the voice.

I am going to need to know more than that before I stop trying to help Ian. I do not know you, but I know you have been very forceful in making sure Brayden and I do not get in touch with Ian right now, Kenzie expresses her true feelings about the visitor in Ian's mind.

Like I said before, I am not going to hurt Ian, and I have been here all along. I have just been out of time, or this timeline, until my mother was presented with a ring a few minutes ago.

What ring?

I am not sure. But when she touched it, I became stronger again, or for the first time, in a long time. I'm not really sure how to explain it. I just know I am supposed to be here, right now. Ian is safe with me, and you have to leave now. Please, let me do this.

That is all Kenzie hears before being pushed out of Ian's mind again, one last time.

"What happened?" Connor asks Kenzie.

"I'm not really sure, but it has something to do with the missing ring, I think," Kenzie replies.

Chapter 10

Kenzie's Mistake?

"Remember Kayla, some of the memories I am about to give you will be true, while others will be fake, only for your protection," Kayla recalls some of what Alexis told her before leaving her with Mason. *Maybe that is why I acted like I didn't recognize the ring. Maybe it is because Alexis knew Mason was going to betray her, and show me the ring. But she didn't want Mason to know the truth about the ring. Alexis really did think of everything. Now, how am I going to get the ring from Mason?* Kayla finishes her thoughts with more hope than before.

Kayla paces back and forth in her bedroom thinking of ways to get the ring, but doesn't know where to start. First, she doesn't know if Mason will have the ring, or if the woman that is with him will have it. Second, whoever will have it, where will they keep it? Third, how is she going to be able to convince either of them to give the ring to her, or for her to find a way to steal it from them? She knows she has to start planning quickly, because she doesn't know if, or when, that woman with Mason is going to leave.

As Kayla paces in her room, Mason and Maria are in his massive office, which is lined with bookshelves that are fully stocked with almost every history book anyone could think of. His office has a large oak desk sitting in front of a sunlit window with no curtains, and two short backed chairs placed in front of the desk. The floor is lined with the most exquisite multi-colored handmade rug, which both Maria and Mason are oddly enough pacing on, the same way Kayla is pacing in her room.

"Could she be lying to us, Mason? It's not like she has any reason to trust us," Maria asks.

"I can assure you that what I have learned about her from all of the time I have spent with her, the reaction we received from her was genuine. There were no facial markers to suggest she was lying, and her body language suggested that she has never seen this ring before we showed it to her," Mason insists to Maria.

"Why would Ian tell us at the school that Kayla gave the ring to him? No one even knows about her, as far as I know, except for the two of us..." Maria's voice softens as she finishes that sentence.

"What is it, Maria? What is on your mind right now?" Mason notices the change in her tone.

"What if this is all a trap? Ian started asking me a lot of odd questions regarding the Believers and the Council, along with information about myself. He even asked questions that involved you, like questions about Connor and Kenzie, now Kayla and this ring. What if he knows I am betraying them all?" Maria is beginning to spin out of control with fear.

"Get ahold of yourself, Maria. There is no possible way Ian can know anything about us working together, considering he just met you. He may have doubts about the Council's ability to keep up with all of the special children in the world, but that would be all," Mason tries to calm Maria down.

Deep down Mason knows that Maria may have a point. He knows that Kayla and Ian have a telepathic connection, which he has told no one about and placed precautions around the building to keep them from connecting telepathically. *It's possible they have come up with a plan to locate her, by outing someone on their side working with me. If that is the case then Maria could be being used as nothing more than a fool.* Mason will need to make sure he keeps some of his thoughts to himself from Maria, for the time being.

"But if I go back now and the ring has already been discovered as missing, and then the ring shows back up at the same time, then that will give it away that I had it. Then they will start with all of their questions. I have to leave the ring here with you. I can never take it back," Maria insists.

"I understand your logic about you and the ring, if it has been discovered missing already. But what if it hasn't been discovered as missing yet?" Mason asks Maria.

"To be honest, that would be the best outcome. If I am there with them when the ring is discovered missing, then they will have no reason to suspect me or question me about it. Since we are on the subject, I think it would be best if I head back to school now. I don't want to raise any undue suspicion and I have already been gone for two days," Maria declares.

"Again, I concur with you. I will keep this ring here in my office safe until we can figure out definitively what meaning it has to everyone, if anything at all," Mason agrees with Maria, while walking her to his office door. "Now, go ahead and head back to the school. You should not be gone for a long period of time, plus you need to find out what has been happening while you have been gone," Mason instructs Maria as she agrees and walks out of his massive office.

Mason closes the door behind Maria, walks over to his office safe, and presses in a six-digit code to unlock it. Once it is unlocked, a light turns green, he then turns the handle on the outside of the safe door, pulling it open. Once the door is open, he places the ring inside next to a few other items, a lock of hair, a journal, some old coins, and an old photo, he has acquired over the years. Mason shuts the safe door and turns the handle back to its locked position until the light turns from green to red.

Now that the ring is securely locked in a safe place, it's time to get back to work. Time to see how the manhunt is coming along for the escaped traitor, Mason thinks to himself as he too exits his office.

***

As Jax and the headmaster conclude their meeting, Jax turns and leaves his office. He does not make it more than one step outside of the door before Brayden is right up in his face rambling on and on. What he is rambling on about Jax does not really understand, yet.

"Brayden! Slow down and start at the beginning. I did not understand a word of what you just said," Jax explains to him.

"Well, Kenzie thought that while you were down here, we could try something with Ian to try to see if we could help him unlock the Time Keeper. Then everything went wrong from there," Brayden starts to explain to Jax.

"By wrong, how wrong?" Jax hates to ask, but does anyway.

"We need to get back up to my room now. I will keep explaining as we go, but we have to go. NOW!" Brayden demands of Jax.

Jax can tell by the look on Brayden's face he is not joking and is very much being serious. This alone makes Jax grab Brayden's arm to start their way up to Ian and Brayden's room. While Brayden continues to explain the situation to Jax, they are on the move towards Ian.

Jax and Brayden make their move through the school lobby, straight to the elevators. To their surprise, one is already open, as if it is waiting for them. They both run into the elevator as Jax begins pressing the button for Brayden and Ian's floor, until the doors shut. The elevator starts its upward motion, while Brayden is filling Jax in on everything that has been happening, neither of them can hear the hum of the belts pulling them up. It is only when they hear the 'ding', they realize they are at their destination and hop off the elevator. They begin their way down the hall to their room.

***

Meanwhile, back in Brayden and Ian's room, Kenzie and Connor are just watching Ian sleep. Kenzie is unsure of what is really going on, but she knows not to try and attempt going back into Ian's mind again. Not right now anyway.

"Do you think Ian is safe?" Connor asks Kenzie.

"To be honest with you, I'm not completely sure. I can say that whoever, or whatever that power is that is in with Ian now, did unlock the Time Keeper and they assured me he was safe. I sort of believe he is safe," Kenzie says to keep Connor relaxed.

"I'm scared for him. How come no one believes he has a friend named Kayla? I believe he does. Just because I have not met her doesn't mean she isn't real," Connor expresses to Kenzie.

"I really don't know, Connor. I have not known any of them very long, but I also believe Kayla is real. I don't know why some people have to see something to believe it. Like, I have never met a lottery winner, but I know they exist. Also, the same as your fear for Ian. I don't have to see it to know your fear is real for him. I think when people grow up, they stop believing in things they can't see, because they think it is childish and only something for kids, like us. When I grow up, I will never stop believing in everything," Kenzie tells Connor.

"Well, we are at this school, and it's supposed to be a school to help kids like us, but they don't believe Ian either. How can they help us if they don't believe in us?" Connor makes a good point to Kenzie.

"I don't know, Connor. Maybe that is why we are here now, to remind them and help them help us," Kenzie says to Connor. Just as Kenzie finishes, Brayden and Jax come barging into the room.

"It's about time you both showed up. We have been sitting here, too scared to do anything. I was not going to try and go back into Ian's mind again, alone anyway," Kenzie tells the pair of them.

"What do you mean 'go back in alone', Kenzie?" Brayden asks before Jax has the chance.

"When I got up here, after leaving you down there in the headmaster's waiting room to wait for Jax, Ian was talking to someone in his sleep. I wanted to see if I could go in and at least talk to Ian, or see who he was talking to. But that did not go as planned," Kenzie stops.

"First, that is not much of a plan. Second, you should never have tried that without us here. Why didn't you let me know what was going on? You could have interrupted that meeting, which by the way, went nowhere," Jax scorns Kenzie.

"I was not sure how to interrupt the meeting, first of all, and I was able to speak to the person that is in Ian's mind now. At least I spoke to him before he kicked me out, again," Kenzie says with some satisfaction. "Would you like to know what he said to me?"

"Don't think that what you did will go without some form of punishment, regardless of the information you gathered. The ends never justify the means. This simply means that no matter how good the outcome is, it does not override the proper way of getting information. Not only could you have hurt yourself, but what about Ian's mind? Or how do you think the rest of us would feel if you hurt yourself by accident? We would all hurt. No information is worth that. Understood?" Jax reprimands Kenzie for her inexcusable use of her powers.

"Yes, I'm sorry. I didn't think about all of that. I just wanted to help Ian," Kinsey apologizes to the group.

"Good, now tell us what you found out, please," Jax asks Kenzie calmly.

"Well, whoever is in Ian's mind with him has been there before, I think. To make things even more interesting, he said he's been there, I guess in Ian's mind, but very weak, until his 'mother' touched a 'ring'. He is not sure about what 'ring', or where she touched it, but he said it is very recent. He also said he can unlock the Time Keeper, but Brayden and I couldn't. He then thanked me for trying to help Ian, and then kicked me out of Ian's mind again. I think this was also the same thing that pushed Brayden and me out earlier, before going to get you, Jax," Kenzie finishes with all she learned from inside Ian's mind. "Oh, I remember one more thing. He also said that Ian is safe with him, and I believe him for some reason."

"It can't be true. There is no way possible for this to be who I think it is," Jax says softly under his breath. In a daze like state, Jax walks over to the bedroom door, steps out, and closes the door behind him, leaving the others alone in the main room.

Chapter 11

The Girl?

Ian is still standing in the same spot, watching the two men, Sebastian and Grayson, fight. This is not like any other fight Ian has witnessed before between two people. This is just a one-sided fight, which Grayson is the only one fighting. Sebastian is hardly even blocking Grayson's punches.

It seems odd to Ian that Sebastian is not putting up much of a fight against Grayson. It looks as if Sebastian thinks he deserves this beating and is allowing Grayson to get it out of his system. He can't be too sure of what his reasoning is, but he is glad to see that Grayson is getting tired of hitting someone that's not fighting back.

Grayson quickly walks over to Sebastian, who is on the ground, and calls him a coward for not fighting back, then turns and stumbles away. As Grayson is leaving Sebastian on the ground in that filthy alley, he tells him that he never wants to see him again, ever.

Ian can tell by the look on Sebastian's face that these words from Grayson hurt him more than the punches he just endured. Sebastian slowly gets up off the grungy ground of the alley and starts making his way in the opposite direction leading out of the alley, from which Grayson had gone. At the end of the alley he exited, turned left and disappeared from Ian's sight.

Ian is not sure why he is still in the alley now that the fight between the two is over, and everyone has left, except for him, or so he thinks. Because it is just then that a little girl comes running out from a small dark corner of the alley.

Ian doesn't say anything to her, but watches her as she runs over to a specific spot in the alley, just past where Sebastian was laying for most of the fight, and pick something up. He has a feeling that she does not belong there in that alley, and what she has picked up is very important. Ian begins to walk closer to the little girl to get a better look at what she has found and to see what she looks like, but suddenly stops. He doesn't have to get any closer to recognize what she is holding in her hands. He knows what it is, because he now wears it on his own wrist. It's the Time Keeper.

"So, this is the fight when Sebastian thinks he lost the Time Keeper, when really it was stolen by this young girl. What purpose would this girl have by taking it, and does she know what it is? I need to know more about her, but how?" Ian speaks out loud in his sleep.

"Jax! Get out here now! Ian is talking in his sleep again, and you are the only other person that knows the history of the Time Keeper," Brayden yells at Jax, who is still in the hallway.

Jax has not completely processed all he has learned from Kenzie's dangerous trip into Ian's mind. Now he's being yelled at about something else?

Jax opens the bedroom door in time to catch Ian still talking in his sleep.

"Why can't I follow her?" Ian asks out loud.

Because this is the last memory Sebastian Helen was able to store in the Time Keeper, a voice inside Ian's mind replies to him.

"I don't understand how this is going to help me find Kayla. All this memory has done is create more questions than answers. How can I find out who this little girl is, and where she is taking the Time Keeper from here?" Ian questions the voice, which he can only hear in his mind.

All I can tell you is that if you believe in something strong enough, you can make anything happen. If you are not a person who believes, then become a believer, is all the voice says to Ian before waking him up.

Ian is slowly opening his eyes and is not shocked to see everyone standing over him in his bedroom with so many different looks on their faces. "How long was I out this time?" he asks.

"Really? That's the first thing you have to say?" Jax says to Ian and not in a happy tone.

"I know you are not happy with me right now, Jax, but seriously, how long have I been out?" Ian asks again.

"You have only been asleep for a few hours," Kenzie tells Ian.

"Well that's much better than a day or two. What happened to the two of you? You both were supposed to come in, once I was asleep and dreaming. Why didn't you?" Ian asks Kenzie and Brayden.

"We did go in after you fell asleep and were dreaming. When we entered your dream, it was one of you and your family on a skiing trip. Brayden and I tried to pull you from the dream, but you had such a strong connection with it, we couldn't. Then I asked Brayden to try harder, but then as we did, someone kicked us out of your mind," Kenzie tells Ian. "Don't you remember any of that?"

"I remember dreaming of the ski trip, then the feeling of being torn apart. It was a pain I had never felt before. On one hand I felt that I needed to leave, but on the other hand, I felt more about staying with that family in the dream. I didn't want to leave them, because they were something I wanted and they were there with me. Then the pain stopped, and I was no longer in my dream but in a memory from the Time Keeper. I thought you both were able to unlock it for me but couldn't come with me. Then the more I thought about it, it made no sense because you have been in a memory with me before," Ian says while looking directly at Kenzie. "You were able to come into the memory I was stuck in for two days of Sebastian and his father."

"You are correct about me being able to go into the memory with you, but you are wrong about us being able to open the Time Keeper. I can assure you that it wasn't us, because I did something foolish while you were asleep. After Brayden and I were kicked out of your mind, we both left Connor here to watch over you while we went down to get Jax. As we sat down there waiting for his meeting to be over, Connor called out to me with his mind.

He was scared because you started talking in your sleep. So, I left Brayden to wait for Jax, and I came up here as fast as I could. Once I came in and heard you talking in your sleep, I wanted to know who you were talking to, so I went in your mind alone. I know now that was a selfish thing to do. While I was trying to get to you, someone, or something, blocked me from getting to you. They said they were able to open the Time Keeper for you and that Brayden and I would have never been able to do it anyway. I think they have been in your mind before, and they said you would be safe with them. Then they pushed me out again. I didn't try that again," Kenzie finishes telling what she did.

"Wow, you risked yourself for me? Thank you, but please don't ever do that again. If anything were to happen to you, because of me, I could never live with myself. Do you promise?" Ian asks Kenzie as she nods back to him. "I'm still not completely sure exactly how, or who gave me access to the Time Keeper. But the memory I accessed is the very last one Sebastian stored in it, before he thought he lost the Time Keeper," Ian tells the group.

"What do you mean, thought he lost the Time Keeper?" Jax asks.

"It was actually stolen from the alley after Grayson and Sebastian's fight. It fell out of Sebastian's pocket so fast I didn't even notice it. After their fight ended, they both went on their separate ways in different directions out of the alley. Jax, the reason Sebastian is unable to find the Time Keeper when he goes back the next day to look for it is because as soon as he left, a little girl came out of a dark corner in the alley and picked it up. She ran directly to the Time Keeper, picked it up, and took off with it," Ian explains to Jax.

"Do you recognize this girl, or the person who was able to give you access to view the final memory of Sebastian?" Jax inquires.

"No, but there is something about the girl that doesn't make sense. Like she was out of place, or time, because she knew exactly when and where the Time Keeper was going to be," Ian explains his feelings of the little girl.

"Why didn't you just follow the girl to see where she went?" Brayden asks this question.

"A voice said I could not go with her because I was accessing the last memory of Sebastian. Then it kept saying things like, 'if you believe in something strong enough, you can make anything happen' and 'if I'm a person who does not believe, then I need to become a believer'," Ian concludes.

"But what are you supposed to believe in? The power of finding the little girl, or the belief that you will get the Time Keeper later, which you already have?" Kenzie is asking questions too.

"Jax, you sure are being quiet. After everything you have heard us talk about, of all the people in this room, I thought for sure the History Teacher would have something to add to the conversation," Ian says to Jax half-jokingly.

"There are a few things I can add to this, but may be hard for you to hear," Jax says to Ian.

"What are you talking about? What do you know that you are not telling the rest of us?" Ian demands to know from Jax.

"I think that the voice is trying to tell you that a Believer took the Time Keeper from the alley. Remember when I told you that we, the Believers, know where the Time Keeper is, but we cannot directly lead the next of your bloodline to it? But we can start rumors, or other things to get the attention of the next in line. I have a feeling this Believer broke this rule and took the Time Keeper to someone else. Maybe they took it to Sebastian's half-sister you have been looking for. That is the only thing I can think of that would explain the little girl's knowledge of where it was then, and what it does, and who can use it. She has to have taken it to his half-sister," Jax is creating an explanation of events.

"So, now you believe me? The story that Kayla told me is real, and his father did have another child, before he had Sebastian," Ian says to Jax with a bitter undertone.

"Yes, Ian. I am beginning to think you are correct. There is something else I need to tell you. I also think that the voice you were talking to in your mind, the one helping you access the Time Keeper and walking you through the memory, is Junior," Jax says calmly to Ian.

"What are you talking about? Junior is gone, Jax, and he's not coming back. I had to watch him vanish right in front of me," Ian replies to Jax's statement with sadness.

"I know, Ian. But the voice also told Kenzie that he has been in your mind before, but he has been very weak. That is until recently, when he says his mother touched a ring. He does not know where, or what ring, but he knows it was placed in her hand. Then he went from being weak to being who you talked to, a strong and powerful voice, someone strong enough to kick Brayden and Kenzie out of your mind, Kenzie twice. The only explanation is that somehow, Kayla has been shown the ring that is now missing, the one that she gives you, or gave you on your eighteenth birthday. Someone has taken it to Mason, and they let her hold it," Jax tries to explain the best he can.

"Then if this is true, and that is Junior, why is Kayla not here with us now? If history is back on track, why is she not here?" Ian asked no one in particular. "But if that was Junior, that would explain the white room I was in. A white room is the way Junior used to communicate with me in the beginning, before he was erased from the future, by Kayla. Before he was able to show himself to me, he used a white room to show me memories, and now that I think about it, the two of you were part of them. He showed me a memory of a little girl and her brother, you two. And you must have frozen Connor for the first time, because he was not moving and you, Kenzie, were scared.

Now that I remember that memory, I am a bit worried, because there is another memory he showed me that has not happened yet, and it does not look good," Ian explains the white room to everyone.

"What exactly did he show you that you are afraid of?" Jax is asking.

"It was a vision of a room that held a group of people, but I couldn't make out the people or the place," Ian explains. "How are we supposed to stop that from happening?"

"If you believe in something strong enough, you can make anything happen. Isn't that what the voice told you?" Connor asks Ian. "Then believe harder than you ever have before, and make it happen."

Chapter 12

The Elevator?

"Ian, I think there is someone I can go speak to and maybe find out more about this girl you saw in the memory and Maria. This does mean that I will have to leave the school for a few days, so will you four be able to stay here without getting into any more trouble? And by trouble, that also means not trying to go back into Ian's mind, for dreams or memories," Jax says to the group.

"Where are you going, and who are you going to see?" Ian inquires.

"Ian, I'm sorry, but that is something I am not allowed to tell you. If I could, I promise I would, but I took an oath that can never be broken. Just know that I would not leave you if I was not sure about this," Jax apologizes to Ian. "Now, can you all stay out of trouble?"

"I will keep an eye on them," Brayden chimes in.

"Ha ha ha! You can hardly watch yourself Brayden, how are you going to be able to watch anyone other than yourself?" Kenzie snaps with a joke.

"That's not true. I can babysit just fine," Brayden dishes the jokes right back to Kenzie.

"That's enough you two. I would feel better knowing Connor was keeping an eye on you three," Jax says while pointing at Brayden, Kenzie, and Ian.

Connor gives Jax a big smile and says, "You got it, Jax!"

"How about if we all keep an eye on each other? Will that make you feel better?" Ian asks Jax.

"Yes, honestly it will. I will feel much better knowing you are all watching out for each other at all times. There are still some things around here that need answers as well. Like finding out where Maria went and if she has the ring with her. I trust you will be able to handle these things?" Jax tells the group.

"We will see what we can find out about Maria here, as long as you are finding out about the girl from the memory and Maria, from where you are going," Ian replies to Jax.

"Now, while I am gone, if anyone asks you where I am, you can tell them you are unaware of my absence. I will inform the headmaster of my unscheduled trip, so if he is asked, he can let anyone know what I tell him of my whereabouts. Okay, I think it's time for us to separate for the time being. This way we are not seen together before I depart," Jax suggests.

"Sounds good. Kenzie, why don't you and Connor go ahead and go down to your room for a while, Brayden and I will stay up here for a bit. Jax, when you leave, think out to Kenzie to let her know you are leaving, so she can let us know. This way we can get together to figure out as much as we can from the library," Ian orders the team.

Everyone agrees with Ian's plan and head their separate ways, for now.

Kenzie and Connor head down to their room, which is only one floor down from Ian and Brayden's, so they will be close at all times.

Jax takes the same elevator with Connor and Kenzie, but continues on after they step off at their floor. The elevator makes a sudden stop, a few floors before his, and to Jax's surprise, as the doors open, there stands Maria with a clipboard in hand.

Maria is shorter than Jax, standing at five foot three inches tall, against his six foot two inches. She has brown hair that hangs a little past her shoulders, she is from New Jersey, which means she has a short fuse and takes no messing around. If she asks a question, she wants the answer.

"Maria, I noticed you left the school pretty abruptly the other day. When did you get back? I hope everything is okay?" Jax makes small talk with her.

"Yes, everything is fine now. There was a report of a child with new powers that may have needed our attention, but it turned out to be nothing," Maria replies back to Jax, covering her true actions of the past two days. "And I just got back a few hours ago."

"Why didn't you tell me about the possible child with powers? I would have gone with you, just in case it turned out to be true and you needed help," Jax digs a little deeper with Maria.

"Jax, if I felt that I needed your help, I would have asked for it. Since I did not ask you to join me, then you should understand you were not needed. Besides, don't you have your hands full with your own bunch of troubled children?" Maria snaps back at Jax.

"I would not call them troubled. I would say they are misunderstood and determined for the truth to be revealed," Jax corrects Maria.

"And what truths would that be? What exactly are you implying, Jax?" Maria asks.

Maria is so consumed with what Jax just told her, she did not hear the loud 'ding' of the elevator as it reached Jax's floor.

"Well, glad to have you back, but this is my stop. If you will excuse me, I have some things I need to take care of at this moment. Have a great evening," Jax says as a goodbye to Maria as he exits the elevator on his floor.

As the doors are closing on the elevator, Jax hears Maria asking, "What truths?" Knowing he has her now thinking of everything, he does not have to worry about her looking for him while he is gone on his trip.

Jax makes it to his room, gathers a few things he will need for a two-day trip, and packs it all in a small backpack. Once he has everything for his trip, it's time for him to head down to the headmaster's office. Jax walks out of his bedroom, shutting his door, making sure the door is locked, then heads over to the elevators.

Jax does not have to wait long for the elevator, and when the door opens, he is pleased to see it is empty. The last thing he wants is to get back on an elevator with Maria.

Now that he has made it to the lobby of the school, he heads over to the headmaster's office to give him a story of his absence as well. He is not in a habit of lying to the headmaster, but telling him the truth could put him in danger, and that is not something he is willing to do.

With everything complete on Jax's end for his departure, he reaches out to Kenzie with his mind, *Kenzie, are you there?*

Yes, I'm here Jax.

Okay, I am leaving now. Oh, and by the way, Maria is back at the school. I ran into her on the elevator and she said she just got back a few hours ago. Her excuse is that she was on Believer business, something about a child with powers that turned out to be false. I think she is hiding something. If you try anything with her mind, she will know, so you will have to snoop the old fashion way.

And what exactly is the old fashion way?

You will have to talk to her and try to trick her into telling you something you shouldn't know. You will need to sneak around and follow her without being seen. I mean you will actually have to spy on her. Now tell the others, and I will be back as soon as I can. Be careful, are the last thoughts of Jax's to Kenzie as he walks out of the front of the school and gets into the car he will be driving to his secret destination, which is unknown to the students or to the headmaster.

***

Kenzie finishes telling Ian everything Jax told her as he was leaving the school for his mysterious meeting.

I will fill Brayden in, and I'll call for you later. I think we should all meet later to come up with an old fashioned way of investigating Maria, and fill Connor in as well. He may come in handy, Ian thinks to Kenzie. He then releases their connection and turns his attention to Brayden.

"Okay Brayden, now we are going to have to revert to Old Fashioned ways of investigating Maria. Do you think you are up to it?" Ian asks.

"It depends on what you mean by 'Old Fashioned'. Are we going to have to wear old clothes or something?" Brayden asks in return for the task that has been set out for them.

"No, why would you think we have to dress in old clothes? Haven't you ever tried to follow someone before without them knowing you were following them?" Ian tries another way to explain Old Fashioned to Brayden.

"Yes, but I gotta wear my own clothes. This sounds like it's going to be a lot of work if we have to keep changing," Brayden confesses to Ian.

Ian spends thirty more minutes explaining everything to Brayden, but by the look on his face, Ian is not sure if he understands it all. "If you don't get it now, you will later. We are going to meet with Kenzie and Connor soon to figure out a plan," Ian finishes with Brayden.

"I get most of it. The only part I don't get is the Old Fashioned part. Are we going to have to dress in old clothes or something to get close to Maria?" Brayden questions.

"Oh, Brayden, you will soon understand, I promise," Ian confirms with him. "Please, relax."

Kenzie, are you and Connor ready?

Yes, we have been waiting on you. What took you so long?

Explaining things to Brayden took a little longer than I expected, but we are ready. Why don't we meet in our last base of operations in the library, the one where Jax came to us?

That sounds like a perfect spot. We will meet you there, Kenzie breaks off with Ian and tells Connor to get ready, because they are headed down to the library.

"You mean I have to study while you all get to do all the other stuff that Jax asked us to do? That's not fair," Connor tells Kenzie.

"No, Connor, you don't have to study. You are going to help us. Ian and I have a secret meeting place in the library. By the way, there is nothing wrong with doing a little studying now and again, or just reading a book for fun. Just saying," Kenzie replies to Connor.

With that, Connor gives his big sister a smile and is up and ready to head to their secret hiding place. They exit their room and head to the elevator and press the down button and wait.

As Kenzie and Connor wait for the elevator, Brayden and Ian are now exiting the elevator on the library floor. Ian leads Brayden through the rows of books to his and Kenzie's last workstation, but she and Connor are not there.

Kenzie, are you and Connor all right? Where are you? Brayden and I thought you two would be here before us, Ian thinks to Kenzie.

We are fine. I had to convince Connor to come with me and that he is not going to have to study in the library. We are just waiting for the elevator to come up and get us.

We should be down in just a few more minutes, Kenzie thinks back to Ian.

As Kenzie finishes her thoughts back to Ian, the elevator doors open and there stands Maria, clipboard in hand. Kenzie is looking directly at her, and her body does not seem to want to get on the elevator with Maria.

"Hello, Kenzie and, Connor is it? How are you both this evening?" Maria asks.

Kenzie is still standing in the same spot and does not answer Maria's questions.

"Is something wrong, Kenzie? Are you both going down?" Maria asks more questions.

"Oh, sorry. Yes, we are going down and we are both doing great. Thanks for asking," Kenzie is finally able to get her answers out to Maria, while she and Connor make their way onto the elevator with Maria. Kenzie is making sure that she is staying between Connor and Maria at all times.

"What floor are you going to?" Maria asks. Before Kenzie can answer, all the floor button lights come on.

"Well, we are headed to the lobby, but it seems this elevator maybe stopping at every floor," Kenzie says while looking at the floor buttons on the elevator wall.

"That's odd," Maria says. "Why don't we hop out of this one and grab the next one? I'm headed to the lobby as well," she suggests.

"Actually, why don't you go ahead and grab the next one? We really don't mind taking this one. Connor loves elevators, and we are in no hurry. Anyway, you never know who may get on at each stop. I'm sure you don't want to be stuck on an elevator with who knows how many kids by the time it reaches the lobby. I bet you have more important things to do," Kenzie insists to Maria, hoping she takes the bait and takes the next elevator, which thankfully she does.

"Yes, I think I will wait for the next one. I am in a bit of a hurry. Maybe we can get together soon and talk more about you and Connor," Maria says as the elevator doors are shutting.

"Yes, that sounds great," Kenzie replies through the closing doors.

After Kenzie is sure the elevator doors are completely closed, and Maria can't hear her, she asks, "Connor, did you do that?"

"Yes, I did that. I decided to press all the buttons so we would not have to tell her what floor we are going to. Ian does not trust Maria, so I don't either," Connor says back to Kenzie.

"Brilliant," is all she can say to Connor in response, before reaching out to Ian to explain their delay.

Ian, we may be a little bit longer than expected. We ran into Maria in the elevator. Don't worry though, it was just for a few minutes. But we have to stop at every floor now on our way to the library, thanks to Connor's quick thinking that is. We are fine, and I'll explain when we get there, Kenzie thinks to Ian, then cuts off the connection before he can reply.

"You are amazing, Connor," she says to him.

The rest of the way down to the library floor, they rode in silence, except for the sound of the elevator's 'ding' at the stop of every floor. At every stop when someone gets on the elevator and notices all the buttons are pressed, with two children in it, they promptly get off just as fast as

they got on. This seems to amuse the two of them
all the way down to their actual floor.

Chapter 13

Secret Destination?

Jax has arrived at his destination. It was only a two and a half hours drive out of the city to the north. He reached a small home, nestled back in a wooded area. It has a long private driveway, made up of rock and gravel, lined with the most beautiful oak trees that branch over the driveway.

Upon reaching the front of the small house, Jax is able to see past the glamour spell which has been placed over the area for its protection, and can actually see the place he once called home. The small house others see has changed into a large castle-like home. This castle-like home is several stories tall, with the most beautiful masonry and stained glass windows, ever to be seen on a home, and they are noticeable through the entire palace. This is the home in which all Believers are raised until they are deemed old enough to be on their own to watch over someone. There is no specific age set for one person or another, so the

Chancellor of the Believers has been here for over two hundred years to oversee the process.

Jax knows that if there is any information about the little girl from the memory Ian was shown of Sebastian and Grayson's fight, which is the last memory Sebastian was able to store in the Time Keeper before it was stolen, that Billie June will be the one with all the answers. She will also hold answers regarding Maria.

Billie June has not always been the Chancellor of the Believers. She once was brought here to be raised as well. She was, and still is, a Believer, but for many years now she has overseen all the Believers. She makes sure, not only are they taught the proper ways of their culture, but also makes sure none of the current Believers break their rules. Any Believer who does not follow proper protocol with their culture has to answer to Billie June. No one has ever said that to be a good thing.

Jax makes his way from the car to the main entrance of the castle-like home from his past. Entering through the gigantic wood doors, Jax feels like he is a kid again, just like when he first came here to live and learn. Everything is newer, of course, but to Jax, it is all still the same. To many people, no matter how much something changes, it will always remain the same for them, good and bad, all the same memories stay with a person forever. As nostalgic as Jax is, he is quickly reminded of why he is there in the first place by a young girl coming up to him.

"May I help you, sir?" the young girl asks so formal.

"Yes, I am here to see the Chancellor, Billie June, please. Could you inform her that Jax is here and needs to speak with her? It's very important," Jax requests of the girl.

"I can do that for you, sir. If you don't mind, could you please take a seat in the sitting room over there?" she asks of Jax while pointing to a large room just off the area they are in now, which is a room Jax knows all too well.

Without a reply from Jax, the young girl turns and walks away.

Jax makes his way into the sitting room, removes his backpack, sets it on the floor beside him, and takes a seat in a large straight back velvet chair and waits.

It is only about a fifteen-minute wait for Jax, after he has seated himself, before a young adult comes into the room. "Are you Jax?" she asks.

"Yes, I am."

"Splendid. Would you come with me, please?" she politely asks.

"May I ask where we are going?" Jax asks while standing, picking up his backpack and placing it over one shoulder.

"I am to take you to your sleeping quarters first. Then once you are settled in, I will come back for you to take you to see the Chancellor," is the reply from his newest guide, without her looking back at him.

"My sleeping quarters? What gives you the impression that I will be staying the night?" Jax asks.

"The Chancellor insists that if you have come all this way, then you will be here longer than just a quick visit. Hence the quarters for your stay," is her reply. "Or should I inform the Chancellor she is mistaken?"

"No, she is correct, as always. Lead the way," Jax instructs the messenger, knowing he should have known better than to question the Chancellor's orders, and off they go.

They walked down a long and wide hallway, until they reach the base of a stone staircase. In the middle of its upward reach, the staircase breaks off to the left and to the right. It is an amazing grand staircase, which Jax also remembers all too well. He remembers he does not much like these stairs, but he also knows this place has no quarters for sleeping on the ground level, nor any elevators. All of the sleeping quarters are on the second floor and above. He will have to take these stairs to and from his quarters, if he is to venture off his floor.

Jax is relieved that they stop only after one flight of stairs. His messenger guide leads him down a new hall, only two doors down from the top of the staircase, and then stops.

"These are going to be your sleeping quarters for the next night or so. Please take a moment to go inside, unpack, and freshen up if you need. I will return shortly to gather you and lead you to the Chancellor's office," she states to Jax, before opening the large wooden double doors, turns and walks away.

Jax turns towards the now open doors and enters his quarters. As he is entering the room, he has a feeling he has been here before. He does not recall ever going into this room as a child while he was living here. Jax takes a moment to shake off this feeling he has so he can take a more detailed look around the room. Jax is mesmerized by how old this room seems.

The room is fairly large with an old, elegant four post, king size bed. The beautiful wood floors are covered by what looks to Jax to be handmade rugs, which keep the furniture from touching its surface directly. Along one wall, there is a large fireplace with eggshell white paint for its trim and mantle, which really stands out to Jax because of the red wallpaper that covers that wall. The Believers Crest is hand painted all across the wallpaper, along with very large paintings of the original Believers. Jax cannot believe that the Chancellor has placed him in their most sacred room, mostly reserved for the highest members of the Council, or the Believers.

Jax moves over to the four-post bed, drops his backpack on one end and then lies down on his back on the other end. To his surprise, he notices the room's exquisite hand-painted cathedral ceilings, covered with angels and other biblical themes. "Such amazing art work here," Jax says out loud, then glances over and sees a modern crystal chandelier hanging from the ceiling.

"What a shame. This room would look so much more authentic with a candle crystal chandelier hanging there," Jax says and stops suddenly. He now realizes why this room looks so familiar to him. "This is the room from one of Ian's dreams, like the one when he first found me. This is the room he described to me from the first dream he was shown that night, after we met in real time," Jax concludes. "How can this even be possible? Two of the dreams Junior showed Ian were of the past, one almost current, and the last one of a future event. What does this room have to do with the Time Keeper's past?" Jax wonders out loud.

There is a knock on the door of his sleeping quarters, which catches him off guard and startles him. So, he shouts, "I'll be right there!"

There is no reply from the other side of the doors, but the knocking had stopped. Jax did not mean to be so loud, but being startled like that, a yell is all that came out.

Jax makes his way over to the double wood doors, takes a moment to compose himself, then opens one of the doors, slowly.

"I am sorry I yelled at you. I was startled by your knock on the door so soon," Jax implies with an apology.

"Oh, would you like me to come back a little later? Do you need more time?" his guide asks.

"No, I'm ready to go now," Jax replies as he walks out of the room and into the hallway, closing the door behind him. "Lead the way."

With those words, his guide turns and begins to lead Jax to the Chancellor's office, or at least that is where they are supposed to be going. First stop, the grand staircase. Jax is pleased to see that she has taken the stairs down towards the ground floor, since his room is only on the second floor. Once they reach the bottom of the staircase, she turns to the right and leads Jax down another hallway. This one is not like the others in the castle-like house. Jax has never seen this hallway before, as it is small and narrow. This looks like a newer addition to the original place he once called home.

At the end of this small and narrow hallway is a single door. The guide knocks on the door, then without an answer from inside, she opens the door slowly, ushering Jax inside. Jax, of course, complies with the non-verbal instruction he is given and enters the room.

"Jax! It has been such a long time. Why have you waited until now to come for a visit?" asks a voice, which Jax recognizes immediately as the Chancellor, Billie June.

The door shuts behind him, so he moves to take a seat in one of the two chairs that are sitting in front of the same old wood desk that has been there for all Chancellors, for Billie June and the ones before her.

"Thank you for seeing me on such short notice, Chancellor. I would not have come if it was not of the utmost importance," Jax begins.

"I'm surprised it has taken you this long to come visit me, Jax. To be transparent with you, I know why you are here. And you are correct," Billie June tells Jax before he can even ask any questions.

"If you already know why I am here, then why haven't you already made this knowledge accessible to me? Why has it remained a secret for so long?"

"Your questions are valid ones, Jax. There is much I have to tell you, for you to truly understand any answer I give you."

"Like what? How long have you known?"

"Let me start with a story about when I was a young girl and was sent here to live and learn, just like you were once, many, many, many years ago. Will you allow me this privilege?" Billie June asks Jax.

"Yes Chancellor, please enlighten me with your story."

"Thank you. You see, I was brought here when I was very young, some would have said an infant. So, I was raised here all my life. I was taught all of the ways and traditions of the Believers, and learned them very fast. Being such a fast study, I was able to watch another Believer who was assigned to one of Ian's ancestors. You may now recognize his name, Jacob Helen?" Chancellor Billie June stops for a reply from Jax.

"Yes, we have just learned that is Sebastian Helen father's name. So, you were paired to learn from his Believer?"

"Yes, then after I was able to learn all I needed, I was assigned to Sebastian himself. At the time of being paired with Jacob's Believer, Sebastian was already an adult man. He had always had a hard time with a best mate of his, Grayson Zimmerman, by the time I was assigned to him. I knew my hands would be full once he had the Time Keeper permanently."

"What do you mean, permanently?" Jax interrupts the Chancellor.

"Well, the Time Keeper only truly accepts the oldest living person of the Hele family bloodline as the keeper, even though the younger ones can store and access their memories in it. They do not get the true power, or access to the Time Keeper, until they are the oldest living person in the bloodline. But you know that Sebastian never gained that power, don't you?"

"I'm not sure exactly what you may be referring to, Chancellor. Could you elaborate a little more for me?"

"That is the reason you are here, is it not? To understand more about Jacob Helen's past? Then that is what I am trying to tell you about. See, before I was released to watch Sebastian on my own, my predecessor revealed something to me that she never told anyone. She told me something of the most importance on her deathbed. She spoke of a previous relationship of Jacob Helen's prior to marrying Sebastian's mother. This earlier relationship was with a woman named Jennifer.

"Jennifer was Jacob's first love, and vice versa. The pair of them fell in love at first sight. Even with a love as true and strong as theirs, Jacob's secrets of his family history upset Jennifer. She believed that with true love between two people, there should never be any secrets. She believed that you love a person as a whole, no matter their past. But Jacob had taken an oath to never reveal anything about the Time Keeper, until a specific time, which he could not break. He was only allowed to share that information once a child was born, conceived between Jacob and his true love, and wife. He tried to explain that all her questions would be answered in time, but she felt she could not marry someone she truly did not know, even though she truly loved him. That is when she ended their relationship. This, in the end, hurt Jacob so much that he packed up and moved away from Jennifer, soon after.

"Jennifer only found out a short time after Jacob had moved away that she was with child. *His* child. By the time she found out, Jacob was already in a new relationship with Sebastian's mother in Danvers, so she never told him.

Now that Jennifer is unwed and with child, she knows she has to find a suitor quickly, which she does with William Waddill. They meet on one of his trips from New York, from picking up a shipment of gold and silver sent from London, which he and his brother-in-law, James Geddy, Jr. sold in Colonial Williamsburg. Colonial Williamsburg was the city capital of Colonial Virginia from the 17th-century to the 19th-century. She moved with him to Colonial Williamsburg on his second trip through her town, because that is when she told him she was expecting his child. She knew he would have to propose and they would have to get married quickly, to save not only her family name, but to save his as well. So, they married in her town and moved the next day.

"Once they settled in Colonial Williamsburg, VA., it was not many months after Jennifer gave birth to a healthy baby girl, which they named Camryn. On Camryn's christening day, William placed a silver ring on Jennifer's ring finger, and explained to her that she was to give this ring to Camryn when she came of age, and Camryn's family line would continue the tradition in perpetuity. . The silver ring had an Ancient Roman inscription inside of it. What William did not know was that a small piece of the Time Keeper was also melted with the silver he used to make that family ring."

"How do you know all of this Chancellor?" Jax interrupts again.

"Because I put that piece of the Time Keeper in the melting pot. I am also the little girl that stole the Time Keeper, instead of letting Sebastian find it, after his fight with Grayson. That is why the ring has special powers as well, and why it works the way it does when it is put next to the Time Keeper. They can feel each other. Both are made for the same family bloodline, but in different ways and for different uses. By the time Camryn was born, and I was able to put part of the Time Keeper in the melting silver used to make the ring, I was unable to return it somewhere so Sebastian could find it. That was because it was discovered that I broke a rule of the Believers, and I was taken away from Sebastian as his Believer. The rule I broke, to anyone's knowledge, was that I let Sebastian lose the Time Keeper. It was not that I stole it and helped create something new for another generation of the Hele family bloodline. I have never told anyone about this, until now," Chancellor Billie June finishes.

Chapter 14

Old Fashioned?

Now that Connor and Kenzie's fun has come to an end, with the elevator making its stop on their intended stop on the library floor, they both seem to be happy that their ride is over. They both run out of the elevator like one of them passed gas in it. The two of them are still laughing about the ones who got on the elevator, then got right back off after noticing all the floor buttons were pressed.

It seems their laughter is loud enough for Brayden and Ian to hear, because Kenzie stops laughing suddenly. After standing there for just a few seconds, she looks down to Connor and says, "Fun time is over." Kenzie then leads him through the rows of books to the secret hiding spot.

Even though Connor may not like to study, he has always loved books. Now, more than ever, since he has powers and is different than other kids, he knows he does not need his powers to read. He reads the same as everyone else, sort of. He does have a little trouble with some words, but he is reading at a second-grade level. One day he knows he will be able to read fast, but he enjoys reading slow until then. Reading slow allows him time to create the story he is reading in his mind, with his power of imagination. He's in awe with all the books in this school's library.

"Finally, you made it," Ian says to Connor and Kenzie as they round the corner of a row of books that opens up to the hiding spot.

"I said it was going to take longer than expected," Kenzie snaps back at Ian.

"You did tell me that. Now why don't you fill us in on what happened with Maria," Ian replies to Kenzie.

"The short version is that once the elevator reached our floor, Maria was already on it. She must have been coming from the Sky Lounge, or your floor, because those are the only two floors above ours. She was on her way down. We got on with her, then she asked what floor we were going to, but before I had a chance to answer, Connor mentally pressed all the floor buttons. He made it look like the elevator was malfunctioning. Since all the floor buttons were lit up then, I told her we were going to the lobby. But unfortunately, so was she. I was able to convince her to take the next elevator, since the one we were on was going to be stopping at every floor. I told her since Connor loves elevators so much, we would just take the one we were on down to the lobby. It worked, and she got off the elevator. As she was getting off the elevator, she did say something about getting together soon with Connor and me to talk about us," Kenzie explains the elevator incident with Maria.

"That does sound like a close call. Way to go, Connor! Quick thinking like that is exactly what we will need for our mission, old fashioned investigation of Maria," Ian boasts at Connor.

"Okay, there it is again, Old Fashioned." If that does not mean old clothes, then what does it mean?" Brayden asks the others.

Ian, Kenzie, and even Connor all look at each other and start laughing.

"It's not old clothes, Brayden. It means that we have to watch Maria in ways that don't involve using our powers on her," Connor explains.

"Then why not just say that? What does Old Fashioned have to do with investigating?" Brayden questions again.

"We are in a library, Brayden, so I suggest you find a dictionary and look up the phrase 'old fashioned' and its meaning. You will find out that it does not only pertain to clothing, or even old clothing for that matter," Ian says jokingly.

"Whatever. Can we get back to Maria, please?" Brayden asks, wanting to change the subject now that he feels a little embarrassed.

"Yes, Brayden. Now Jax said that he felt Maria is hiding something. We cannot use our powers on her to find out what that may be, because she will know as soon as we try them on her. So, since we can't use powers on her, that does not mean we can't use them in other ways. I think we should split up into two groups. Kenzie, remember the other day when we came back from the Bed Bath & Beyond, and we ran into Brayden in the elevator? Well, I was thinking that if the moment came available, then we should get into Maria's room and see if Jax was telling the truth about not knowing she left. This will also allow us to see if she took the ring, of course, and see if we can find out who she is working with. So, what I plan is one group will be to keep a close eye on Maria, and the other to go break-in and snoop around in her room.

Connor, you and Brayden are in charge of getting into Maria's room to snoop around. Since you can move things with your mind, a door lock should be no problem for you, after a little practice. Kenzie and I will locate Maria and follow her. Kenzie may not be able to get into Maria's mind, but she can get into other people's minds to see if they have seen or spoken to Maria," Ian commands the group.

Kenzie could slip into Maria's mind if she wanted to, but once she did, Maria would know that Kenzie was there, in her mind. Doing that would give away the advantage they have over her now.

Everyone looks very happy with their partner and their assignment.

"Kenzie and I will go look for Maria first. We want to make sure we have eyes on her before you two sneak into her room. Once we locate her and the coast is clear for you two, Kenzie will reach out to you, Brayden, and let you know. Connor, until we find Maria, why don't you practice locking and unlocking a door from the outside here in the library? Maybe try a closet door or something. We don't want you accidentally blowing her door up," Ian says while give Connor a smile and wink.

"You may be right. Practice does make perfect," Connor replies to Ian with a smile as well.

Ian and Kenzie go ahead and leave Brayden and Connor to practice locks, while they head to the elevators. "The only obstacle in our way right now is making it to the lobby without seeing Maria before then," Ian tells Kenzie.

"Well, I would say the odds are against us," Kenzie replies.

"Why do you say that?"

"So far today, Jax has run into Maria on the elevators and so have Connor and I. It's like she is just riding the elevator up and down, trying to be alone with us," Kenzie suggests.

"You make a very good point. I don't think it is a coincidence that the three of you have already run into her on the elevators. I say we take the stairs down to the lobby. We are only on the fifth floor, so the stairs shouldn't be a challenge. This way we will avoid a run in with Maria on the elevators," Ian suggest.

"That's a good idea, because no one uses the stairs," Kenzie responds. "Well almost no one, there is the occasional health nut that takes the stairs for fun."

Ian and Kenzie walked over to the stairwell door, which has a sign on it that says "Emergency Exit Only," but they are going to use the stairs anyway.

No alarms sound as Ian pushes the fire exit door open that leads to the stairwell. They both walked in and both flashback to the first time they met.

"This is a lot different than the stairwell at your apartment in Brooklyn. The stairwell there has carpet, and the steps are shorter," Kenzie tells Ian.

"Oh, that's right. Your first trip to Brooklyn, and you ended up in the stairwell of my apartment building. Everyone froze in the hallway, except me," Ian starts laughing.

"Right, and we had to get them into your apartment so the neighbors wouldn't see. Then once inside, we had to tie Jax down because he was so light he was floating," Kenzie replies. "Even with me sitting on him"

"That all seems like it was such a long time ago, with everything that has been happening since then, even though it has only been a little over a month. This reminds me of how precious time is. Time with friends, family, and even those you may not like at the moment. As we have seen, things can change from good, or bad, with just a different choice in a person's life," Ian feels compelled to tell Kenzie.

"Kind of like how Kayla was here, and now she isn't? Also, Connor and I want you to know that we believe she is real. We want you to get her back, so we can meet her," Kenzie expresses to Ian.

Ian gives her a smile and before they know it, they are already at the lobby floor exit.

"Kenzie, can you use your power to get into someone's thoughts, without seeing them? I know you can by knowing that person, but what if you don't know the person or see them. Can you detect someone's thoughts inside the lobby without seeing them? This way we can get an idea if Maria is in the lobby or not before we exit," Ian asks.

"No, I am unable to feel a connection to a mind of someone I cannot see, or haven't seen before. Maybe you can crack the door open just a little so I can see at least one person. I would hate to try my first random mind jump and accidentally end up in Maria's mind," Kenzie admits her fears to Ian.

"Okay, that does sound risky and your plan sounds much safer. Get ready, because I am only going to be able to barely crack open the door and it will only be for a split second. So, you will have to look fast," Ian instructs Kenzie. "Ready?"

"I'm ready," she replies as she takes a stance beside the door. She keeps her face as close to the door as possible without being hit by it when Ian opens it.

Ian grips the door handle, gives Kenzie a look of 'ready?' which she nods back 'yes!', then he pulls it open very slowly and not very far.

Even though Ian opens the door slowly and just for a small crack, Kenzie feels a rush of wind hit her eyes as the door cracks open. The wind rushing in blinds her for a split-second. She blinks quickly, and just as Ian is closing the door back, she catches a glimpse of a boy walking by in a blue shirt. Before she can get the boy's image out of her mind, she quickly reaches out and makes a connection with his mind.

Once Kenzie is in the boy's mind, she is able to do a quick scan of his most recent thoughts. These thoughts include people he has either passed or spoken to, and with luck, no sign of Maria. Just to be on the safe side, Kenzie makes a jump over to a girl standing at the front desk. "River Kate, what a pretty name," Kenzie says out loud to Ian in the stairwell. That is the girl's name whose mind she is in, and again with luck, no sign of Maria in her thoughts either. Kenzie can tell by the girl's thoughts that she has been down in the lobby for some time. "Okay, the coast is clear. No signs of Maria from two different students out there," Kenzie tells Ian.

"Wow, you were able to not only get into one student's mind in that short glance through the crack in the door, but actually two minds?"

"Well, I want to make sure we are in the clear. The last girl, River Kate, has been in the lobby for the longest time. She seems to talk to everyone. She's very nice, which I think we can use to our advantage. When you open the door, follow me and let me do the talking, okay?" Kenzie asks Ian.

"I trust you, Kenzie. Let's go." Ian opens the door and lets Kenzie walk through first, then follows her lead.

Kenzie steps out of the stairwell with Ian in tow, and heads straight for a girl that is standing at the front desk.

"Hello, are you River Kate?" Kenzie asks the girl standing at the front desk.

"Yes, I am. Can I help you?" replies River Kate.

"Sorry to bother you, but I'm new here and my P.E. teacher, Ms. Pam said that if I had any questions about Ms. Carol's basketball tryouts, to come to you. So, that is why I'm here. I hate to be a bother, or any trouble," Kenzie tells River Kate.

"Oh, you are no bother to me at all. I will be more than happy to help you," River Kate starts explaining the schedule to Kenzie. "Did you know that basketball was first created in 1891, by James Naismith? It's a fascinating story actually. He created the game and it only had thirteen rules. That's it, just thirteen. The very first basketball game was played on December 21, 1891. Isn't that awesome?"

While Kenzie is getting the rundown on the basketball schedule and basketball history, she reaches out to Ian's mind, *Why don't you go look around and see if you spot any sign of Maria? I will stay here for a few more minutes letting her tell me about Ms. Pam and Ms. Carol, and more about James Naismith. Then I will come over to you.*

Sounds risky, but okay. Don't stay too long gossiping, Ian thinks back to Kenzie before excusing himself from River Kate and Kenzie.

Ian slowly begins to scan the lobby of the school, not seeing much of anything interesting. There are a few different seating areas. One of these areas is located in the middle of the lobby, with a large half-circle couch in it. The two other areas are smaller and at each end of this area of the lobby. One of the smaller areas has just two chairs at the entrance, and the other at a side entrance, which has a straight couch with two chairs and a coffee table. Maria is not in any of these sitting areas.

Ian is heading towards the elevators, but right before he gets to the elevators, there is an opening that leads into another area of the lobby. When he reaches this area, Kenzie grabs him by his elbow.

"I hope you were going to wait for me before going back there," she said to Ian.

"I can't say that I was. But now that you are here, would you like to join me for a quick peek?" Ian honestly tells Kenzie.

"I told you I would not be long. Yes, I would like to go find out if Maria is back there," Kenzie snaps back.

"Would you like to lead the way, since you are the one that came up with a way for us to get out of the stairwell without being seen?" Ian asks Kenzie.

"Really?"

"Yes, really. I told you that I trust you, and I'll follow your lead," Ian reconfirms to her.

With a big grin she turns and takes the lead, as Ian had suggested. She slowly leads them towards the elevators, then quickly turns right into the opening that leads into the other area of the lobby.

Just as they enter the new area, they both hear Maria's voice. She is talking to someone. Ian and Kenzie are not sure if she is on the phone, or speaking with someone in person. There is a bookshelf dividing them from the entrance to where she is sitting, so they can only hear her. They wait for Maria to stop talking to see if they can hear another voice, but they don't. They assume she is on the phone.

Now that they assume she is alone and talking to someone on the phone, they begin to listen as closely as they can to what she is saying. *Maybe she will say something we can use, to trick her into telling us something,* Kenzie thinks to Ian.

"I already told you. I have not been able to get with any of them to find out what they know, or may think. Jax was very evasive, and the entire incident with Connor and Kenzie was completely unexpected. I have been unable to find Ian or Brayden yet, but I have a feeling Connor or Brayden are going to be the only ones who may reveal something. I'm going to stay down here in the lobby for another thirty minutes to see if Connor and Kenzie get off the elevator, or if I can see Brayden. I will call you as soon as I find out what they know," Maria finishes her conversation and hangs up the phone.

Okay Brayden, you and Connor are up. You will have about thirty minutes to get in and out of her room. We have eyes, or ears, on her now, and she just finished a phone call. She is definitely hiding something. Reach out to me if you have any problems and I'll let you know if anything changes down here. Is Connor ready? Kenzie things to Brayden.

Yes, he is ready. We will head to her room now. Keep a close watch on her, Brayden thinks back to Kenzie. He then tells Connor it's their turn.

"They have eyes, or ears, on Maria, so it's now our turn to see what we can do. Are you ready?" Brayden asks Connor.

"As ready as I can be before breaking into a teacher's room," is Connor's response. That is all Brayden needs to hear to get them out of the library and onto their mission.

Chapter 15

Ears on Maria?

"Are you ready?" Brayden asks Connor.

"You bet I am! Let's go."

Brayden and Connor make their way to the elevators. Once they reach the elevator doors, Connor uses his power to press the up button.

"Practice makes perfect," Connor tells Brayden with a smile.

"Showoff," Brayden replies with a smile as well.

The elevator doors open, and they make their way inside the elevator. Before Brayden can press any buttons, Connor has already taken care of that as well. Brayden just shakes his head at him.

The elevator starts its ascent up to the floor where the head faculty's living quarters are. Maria's room is not on the same floor as Jax's, being that she is Head of the Believers.

Knowing Maria is down in one of the sitting areas in the lobby, their only obstacle now will be getting off the elevator on her floor without being seen or questioned by any other teacher whose room maybe on the same floor as Maria's.

We are about to get off on Maria's floor. Is the coast clear? Brayden thinks to Kenzie.

Yes, we still have ears on Maria. She is not going anywhere for at least twenty to thirty minutes. Good luck and be careful.

Will do, over and out.

The elevator stops with its loud 'ding' and the doors open. As the elevator doors are opening, Brayden and Connor stand very still. To their surprise, the hallway on this faculty's floor is clear.

Brayden and Connor exit the elevator and run down to Maria's door. It only takes Connor two quick seconds to unlock her bedroom door and open it for them to enter.

Now that they are both inside Maria's room, Brayden quickly shuts the door and locks it himself.

"Good job on the lock and door, Connor."

Before Connor can reply to Brayden, there is another voice in the room. "Yes, very good job indeed, Connor. Who knew you had that type of power?"

To their surprise, the voice they are hearing is Maria's!

"Don't be scared. I am not going to turn you both in for breaking into my room."

"You're not?" Connor asks.

"Of course not. Why would I do that? That would ruin the whole plan I have in store for you two," Maria announces to them. "Oh, and don't bother trying to contact Kenzie either. This room has a shield around it, blocking all powers from being used once inside. Nothing in, nothing out."

Brayden takes a stance in front of Connor, the same way Kenzie did when she and Connor ran into Maria on the elevator, making sure he is between him and Maria at all times.

"How did you know we would break into your room?" Brayden asks Maria.

"There is not much I don't know about all of you and what you are going to do. I am surprised about Connor having powers though. That seems to be a detail that has been left out of the information I have received."

"Well, who are you getting your information from? I would be more than happy to correct them," Brayden spits out to Maria.

"That is none of your concern."

"Ian and Kenzie will notice you are gone now from the lobby sitting area, and they will know we are in trouble. Then they will be right up here to get us."

"Don't be so sure about that. You must know by now that they don't actually see me down in the lobby sitting area, they merely hear who they think is me. By the time they realize I have set a trap for the two of you, we will already be gone."

"What do you mean gone?" Connor asks surprised.

"Just away from the school. Like I said before, I am not going to hurt you. I need you both for something I have planned for later. The others will understand soon. Oh, and by the way, you will both fall asleep in just a moment. Let's just say I have some added protection to my room, one being a spell causing you to fall asleep."

Brayden looks quickly back at Connor, who is already falling to the ground asleep. As Brayden turns back to face Maria and make a move towards her, he too is taken over by the spell and falls to the ground asleep.

***

"And you have been holding on to this secret ever since?" Jax asks Chancellor Billie June.

"Yes. You are the only person I have ever told about this. I thought this would be something that I would never have to reveal, but my telling you may be the only way to right my wrong."

'What do you mean, right your wrong? It sounds to me like you did the right thing, as a Believer. You wanted to make sure Sebastian's half-sister would always be a part of her family's bloodline, knowing about it or not. The only wrong doing I can see is the Heads of the Believers, at that time, removing you from watching over Sebastian."

"I can't blame them for removing me, Jax. I knew what I was doing and knew it was forbidden. But I did what I felt in my heart was the best thing to do. I don't believe my actions were wrong, but I do believe that for me not telling anyone what I did back then was wrong. If I would have been up front and honest about what I did then, and why I did it, Sebastian may have been able to find the Time Keeper before it was too late."

"You mean that Sebastian may have been able to go back and repair his and Grayson's friendship, and none of this would be happening now? You can't know that for sure. There are some things that are just meant to be."

"You are correct. But my choice to keep a secret, instead of telling anyone the truth then, has caused many problems for both family bloodlines. It is my fault the two bloodlines become friends, only to become enemies later in life, since Sebastian was unable to make things right between him and Grayson after that fight. I am only telling you this now because I need your help to repair the past. I went to Ian once to seek his help. But when I saw him, on that subway train headed to meet you, I felt so much pain and shame for causing all of this for him, I vanished before he could see me."

"And how am I going to be able to help? Ian is the only one who can access the Time Keeper, but not until he is eighteen. The only way he has had access so far has been by someone named Junior. And Junior had to manipulate time for Ian to even have access to the Time Keeper in the first place. Now Junior maybe back in the future's timeline, now that Kayla's touched the ring that we are sitting here talking about."

"I have an idea about that and also what Ian can do to correct it all. But we can talk more about it tomorrow. I am feeling a bit tired right now," Chancellor Billie June relays to Jax. "If you don't mind, I think I will go and lie down for the evening."

"Yes, tomorrow will be fine. Before I go, is there anything you can tell me about Maria, the Head of the Believers now?"

"Oh what has she done now? Yes, there are some things I can tell you about her, but again, they will have to wait until tomorrow."

"Thank you Chancellor, I can see myself out and back to my room. This will give me some time to work on a few other things." Jax is thinking of trying to figure out what the room he is staying in has to do with any of the things going on now.

Jax stands up and bids his goodbyes for the evening to Chancellor Billie June, before walking out of her office.

Jax then begins his journey back to his room. He begins with the long walk down the small hallway leading from the Chancellor's office, opening up into the great lobby of the place he grew up to become a Believer. Jax does not have a clear mind to notice all the changes around the lobby, much less all the new young Believers that are roaming about the floor.

How can any of this be happening? This is not what I had planned when I decided to come seek the Chancellor's advice. How can she be the little girl, and what does she know about Maria? Jax thinks to himself.

Before Jax realizes it, he reaches the base of the grand staircase and begins to make his way up to his floor, which luckily is only the second floor.

Before Jax knows it, he has made it all the way to his sleeping quarter's doors. He grasps the brass handle, gives it a little twist, and pushes one of the large wood doors open. With his mind still trying to understand everything Chancellor Billie June has told him, he walks over and takes a seat in one of the two straight back chairs that are sitting upon a handmade rug in the room.

Just as Jax is almost completely relaxed, he is startled by hearing Kenzie's voice inside his head. Her voice caused him to shoot up out of the chair and rush over to the bed and grabbed his backpack.

I'm on my way! He thinks back to Kenzie before making his way out of his magnificent, grand bedroom, down the hallway, quicker than he has ever made it down the staircase. He heads straight through the lobby and out of the front doors of the Believers' home. He left without leaving any message or goodbye for the Chancellor. He figures he will have to either come back to get the rest of the answers he seeks or call her to see about getting the information from her over the phone.

***

"Something doesn't feel right about this," Kenzie tells Ian.

"What do you mean?"

"I'm not exactly sure, but I have this feeling in the pit of my stomach telling me something is wrong."

"Have you tried to reach out and check on Brayden and Connor to see how they are doing?"

"No, but I will do that now,"

Brayden? Can you hear me? Connor? Is everything going okay? Answer me! Kenzie thinks to the other pair, but there is no response.

"Ian, I can't connect with either of them. It's like I am being blocked. It feels sort of like when Junior kicked me out of your mind, then blocked me from coming back in."

"Are you sure? Maybe they can't answer you right now for fear of being caught?"

"With their thoughts? No, I am sure something is really wrong here," Kenzie says to Ian as she makes a dash around the row of books that has been blocking them from Maria's line of sight. She is surprised to find that the table in the room is empty. Maria is nowhere in the room to be found. There is just a speaker phone sitting on the table.

"Kenzie, wait, what are you doing?"

"She's not here, Ian! Maria has tricked us. This has all been a trap! We have to go warn Brayden and Connor now!"

"Dang it! Okay, let's go! You keep trying to connect to their minds while we head up to her floor."

"Should I tell Jax?"

"Not yet. Let's first make sure something is wrong. Then, if there is something wrong, you can contact Jax."

"Fine, I'll keep trying to connect with them then."

Ian and Kenzie make their way to the elevators though the lobby, now unafraid of being seen. As they make their way around the couch and other students, they stop and hit the up-call button for the elevator. During the entire short trip through the lobby, Kenzie continues to try to connect to either Brayden, or Connor, but to no avail.

Once they are in the elevator, before Ian can press any floor button, Kenzie grabs his arm and pulls it out.

"What are you doing? Did you get ahold of them?"

"No, but I can tell you they are no longer here at the school now. They are gone. Maria has taken them somewhere else."

"What do you mean?"

"I'll fill you in later. Right now I need to get Jax back here and fast!" Kenzie exclaims to Ian with a tear from her frowning, sad, scared face.

Jax? Maria has Brayden and Connor. She has somehow taken them away from the school. We need you back here right away! Please? She has my baby brother.

Chapter 16

Should We Wait?

After being locked in her room for what seems to be an entire day, Kayla is awakened by a knock on her bedroom door.

"Who is it?" Kayla asks in a very loud shout, without getting out of her bed. To her surprise there is no answer. Unhappy with the lack of response, Kayla climbs out of her comfy bed and stomps over her bedroom door and says, "I said, who is it?"

"Open the door, Kayla. I will not ask again."

Kayla knows by the tone in Mason's voice that he is not joking. Without another word, Kayla unlocks her bedroom door and slowly opens it for Mason. She can tell by the tired look in his eyes that his search for the missing traitor has not gone well.

"So, how was your day?" Kayla asks Mason sarcastically.

"I'm sure you can get a feel of how it went. We have searched every inch of this place, and there is no sign of that traitor. We have watched all the surveillance video and spoken to the two guards he overtook in the elevator, but no trace of how he even left here. It's as if he is the luckiest person in the world, to be able to have passed every camera and not have been seen by anyone, or he simply just vanished. I don't believe either of those to be the truth."

"Sounds to me like you are starting to lose your grip on reality. Once you are unable to tell the difference from what is true and what isn't, maybe it's time to change your ways. Have you ever thought about that? You know? Changing your ways?"

"What makes you presume to know me well enough to assume I have ways that need to be changed? You don't know me. You only know the part of me I have allowed you to see."

"Then from the parts of you that you have allowed me to see, those are the ones that you need to change. You have held me against my will as a prisoner. You have a pack of followers that will do anything you tell them to do, no questions asked no matter what you ask of them. You really do not even ask, you demand of them. Those are things you can change, if you want to."

"Enough! I am not here to discuss what you may think about me, or changes you think I need to make in my life. I came here because you have been in this room all day, and I figured you may want to get out of your room for a bit. Now if I am mistaken, I can always come back at another time."

"No, you are right. I am sorry. I have no place to judge you, or anyone else. So, what do you have in mind?"

"Maria called and said she has a surprise for me, and I want you to be there when she arrives."

"What kind of surprise?"

"She did not tell me, so we will both be surprised when she arrives. Now, let's go get ready for her arrival," Mason orders Kayla. "Do you need to change clothes or anything before you leave your room?"

"Nope, I'm good so lead the way."

Mason takes the lead and ushers Kayla out of her bedroom first, as in 'Ladies First'. Once she passes him, he follows her out of her room, while pulling her bedroom door closed.

Mason walks ahead of Kayla, on their way to the entrance of his hideout to wait for Maria's arrival. They both take a seat, opposite each other, in the sitting area at the entrance and wait.

As they wait for Maria's grand entrance, they make no small talk. They make no conversation at all. The two of them sit in silence. They are both lucky enough not to have to sit in silence for too long before Maria arrives.

***

Maria pulls up to the front entrance of Mason's hideout. As she exits the car, she orders two guards that are standing at the entrance, to pick up her guests, Brayden and Connor. Both of them have been asleep since they were knocked out by the magical spell Maria has placed on her room. She cleverly had that spell in place just in case anyone tried to break in, as they had done.

The guards managed to grab them both and carry them, walking behind Maria, as they make their way into Mason's lair.

"Well, I am glad you are both here to greet me. As you can see, I come bearing gifts," Maria announces to Mason and Kayla.

"I see. I understand the need to grab Brayden, but why in the world would you grab the Green's boy, Connor? He is nothing more than an ordinary child. He can serve us no purpose," Mason asks.

"You mean to tell me that the all-knowing and almighty Mason doesn't know about Connor?"

"How dare you speak to me that way? I am not exactly sure where you are going with this, but you will not address me in any other manner than one with respect. Do you understand me?"

"Yes, I'm sorry to sound like I was being anything other than respectful. If you will allow me to explain."

"Please, do explain yourself."

"Connor is no ordinary child, as you have been led to believe. Connor has the ability to move things with his mind. He has telekinesis."

"And just how are you aware of this power?"

"He used his powers to break into my room a few hours ago. He used his gift to unlock my bedroom door and then push my bedroom door open. I know it was him, because the other one, Brayden, told him he did a great job."

"Really? Now that is the best news I have heard all day. He could be useful if we can convince him to join our side."

"That shouldn't be a problem, since he is so young, he will be easy to convince what we are doing is what is best."

"That may be harder than you think," Kayla chimes in. "Being young does not mean he will believe what you tell him. You just may find it very difficult to change a person's mind, no matter their age."

"Thank you for your input, Kayla, but I have a way of making people see things my way, if you haven't noticed," Mason shoots back at Kayla.

"Can we get back to the guests, please? Do you have a place your guards can put them for their stay here with you?" Maria asks. "It will need to be a room with a few special additions added to it for our protection."

"Of course, Maria. Guards, please carry our guests down to the holding cells in the basement. I hope the two of you will be able to manage two sleeping children to the cells, unlike the last guards who were overtaken by one traitor."

"Yes, sir. I am sure we can handle this task on our own," replies one of the guards, as they both turn and begin their walk down the hall to the elevator, which they will use to take Brayden and Connor to the basement holding cells, to detain them.

"Now that they are taken care of, what exactly are your plans with them? They better be some amazing plans for you to be bringing this much heat on us. You know as well as I do that Jax and the others will stop at nothing to get them back," Mason says, while looking directly at Maria.

"I do. But I would rather us discuss these plans alone. I don't feel it is wise to reveal too much in front of HER," Maria replies to Mason while pointing at Kayla.

"You don't have to worry about Kayla, Maria. I thought we have already been through this. But if it's the only way to get you to clue me in, I will agree to your terms."

Without any instructions or orders from Mason, Kayla starts her way back to her room. "Don't worry, I know my way back. I don't need an escort."

"Fine. This is your chance to earn my trust. Please, go to your room and make no stops anywhere along the way. Maybe, just maybe, if you do this, you might be able to have a little more freedom around here. Understand?"

"Yes, I understand. To my room and nowhere else. I'm sure I can handle that," Kayla said as she has already begun her walk down the hallway to her room.

"Now that Kayla is gone, where would you like to discuss your plans for our new guest?"

"What room is the most secure room you have here?"

"The control room. There is also a conference room set up in there, just for these purposes."

"Then that is where we need to go, now. Once we are in the control room and I am sure we are secure, I will fill you in on what I am thinking."

"Then let me lead the way."

***

Finally. I actually get to walk somewhere without a guard escort, Kayla thinks to herself on her way to her room. But before she can enjoy her time alone, she stops dead in her tracks in the middle of the hallway.

"Don't be afraid, Kayla," she speaks out loud to herself.

"What is going on here?" she asks herself back.

"It's me. The friend that told you about Sebastian's half-sister, in the restroom, except I was using the guard's body," comes her reply.

"Where have you been? I have so many questions for you. I don't even know where to start."

"All of those questions will have to be put on hold for this visit. Right now, I need to use you to gain access to Mason's office, before you get to your room," the traitor who helped her before replies with her voice.

"Are you kidding me? Do you know what will happen to me, NOT you, if I do not go straight to my room?"

"Yes, but you will have to trust me. You, or we will not be caught, but this has to be done in order to set history back on the correct path. Please, don't fight me on this, it will only slow you down."

"I swear if you get me in trouble, I will out you to Mason. I don't know how, but I will find a way, so help me."

***

"Okay, Maria, now that we are here, care to start explaining what you have planned?" Mason asks as he shuts the door to the conference room in the control room.

Maria is walking around the room, looking under lamps, behind paintings, and even under the table.

"What are you looking for?"

"Microphones, or any other type of listening devices. You are not the most trusting person, Mason. I am just making sure we are completely alone in here."

"You might be correct about me being an untrusting person, but I can assure you we are the only two people who will hear what is said in this room. Now get on with it."

"Okay. Now I honestly did not plan on grabbing both of the boys, Brayden and Connor, but I had no choice. I had a feeling they all were up to something, so I set a small trap for them. I created a diversion in the downstairs lobby of the school, because I knew that they were watching my every move. I just did not know who was going to be watching and who was going to be sneaking into my room. I waited in my room to see who the lucky one was, and low and behold, it was those two. I did not know Connor even had any gifts either, until they broke into my room. To be fully transparent with you, I only wanted Brayden. I figured after my last visit here that with Brayden's ability to dream walk, we could use him to get into Kayla's mind and see just how much she really knows. I have a feeling she is just as untrustworthy as you are."

"I have to say, I agree with you, Maria. Now, just how are you going to be able to do all of this without Kayla knowing it was done and getting Brayden to do it in the first place?"

"Glad you asked. Since Brayden didn't come alone to break into my room, and we now have Connor as well, Brayden will do whatever we ask him to do to protect Connor. I have seen the way he has been bonding with Connor and there is no way he will ever let harm come to him."

"Maria. It seems like I made the right decision on getting rid of Kenzie and Connor's parents so you could become head of the Believers, instead of their mother."

"Of course you did the right thing. I am the only one that is willing to do what is necessary to get the job done."

***

"Did you get ahold of Jax?" Ian asks Kenzie.

"Yes, and he is on his way now."

"Now, do you want to explain to me how you know that Maria has taken Brayden and Connor from school?"

"I know because for a while I was unable to connect to either of their minds. I was unable to because I could not feel them. Then as we were getting on the elevator, I became able to feel their minds, but they were very weak, so I was unable to actually connect to them. It's like they are either asleep or being protected by a spell. That leaves only one option, which is Maria, to have taken them."

"But why would Maria take them? More importantly, who would she take them to?"

"I will give you one guess, but I'm sure you already know the answer to your own question."

"Mason!"

"Bingo. You were right to have your suspicions about Maria from the beginning, just as Jax did when he left the school."

"What are we going to do while we wait for Jax to get here?" Ian asks Kenzie.

"I say we go up to Maria's room and see if there is anything we can find out, now that we know for sure that she is gone."

"Sounds like a plan to me. Let's get a move on. I don't care who sees us now," Ian tells Kenzie, as he leads her back onto the already open elevator.

The elevator doors close and begin its upward move towards Maria's room.

As they ride up to Maria's floor, Kenzie tells Ian, "We need to be cautious, because we don't know how she was able to knock Brayden and Connor out cold. We don't want the same thing to happen to us when we get into her room."

"You sure are smart for your age. How do you know so much?"

"Like I said before, Cooper Schools may be in a small Texas town, but they are very advanced. There have been several very influential people who have graduated from Cooper Heigh School."

"I can only imagine. If they are all as smart as you are, then the teachers there must be doing a great job."

Just as Ian finishes his sentence, the elevator doors open on Maria's floor. The two of them stepped off the elevator and into the hallway. They are alone on the floor, so they run down to Maria's room. To their surprise, her door is slightly open. They are about to step into her room, when Kenzie stops again, like before they got on the elevator for the first time.

"What is it?" Ian asks Kenzie.

Kenzie is just standing there and does not answer Ian's question.

Jax? Are you calling for me? She is thinking.

Yes. I want to let you know that I am on my way there, but I don't want you two doing anything until I get there. Is that understood?

So, would that include going to Maria's room and searching for it? We know she is not here, and this is the perfect time to find out what Brayden and Connor were unable to tell us. We may even be able to find some clues as to where she has taken them.

Do not go into Maria's room. Wait until I get there. Kenzie? Do you hear me? Jax is thinking as hard as he can to her.

"Sorry, what were you saying, Ian?"

"I asked what's going on that made you stop."

"It was Jax. He said he was on his way and for us not to do anything until he gets here."

"And what do you think we should do?" Ian asks Kenzie.

***

"Mason, I need to get back to school before they sound the alarms, and I am unable to even get back on campus," Maria tells him, as she's walking out of the conference room. "Take care of our guests until I return."

***

Kenzie! You and Ian better not be going into Maria's room until I get there! It could be a trap for the both of you. I will be there shortly. Please wait!

***

"I say we are already here, the door is already open, so let's go in," Kenzie replies to Ian.

"Let me go in first, so I can make sure there are no more traps," Ian tells Kenzie as he walks past her and through Maria's open door. Once he is in, Ian motions for Kenzie to come on in, signaling the coast is clear.

Kenzie walks through the door, then all of a sudden, the door slams shut behind her.

"Ian, what do we do?" Kenzie shouts, then looks over at Ian just in time to see him falling to the floor. "Ian," are Kenzie's last words, before she also falls flat on the floor.

Jax, we should have listened to you, Kenzie thinks right before she is out cold.

Now that Ian and Kenzie are both trapped in Maria's room, their only hope is that Jax makes it back to the school before Maria does.

Epilogue: Council's Meeting Begins

Now that the heads, or selected, leaders are sitting in silence at the table in the Council's meeting hall, the Council Leader begins with the introductions.

"First, I would like to thank you all for coming. I would not have called a meeting of this magnitude if it were not of the utmost importance. But before I get started on why I have asked you all here, I believe some introductions are in order. For those who do not know King Preston and his brother, Prince Payton of the Embers, they are sitting here to my right."

The brothers do not stand, nor say a word to anyone, as they are merely wanting to find out who the mystery guest is.

"Now, sitting on my left. First, we have Emma selected to represent the Fairley Folk. As they have no one true leader, she is accompanied by Rose," the Council Leader continues.

Unlike the King and Prince of the Embers, Emma and Rose both stand and greet the others sitting at the table with a simple smile and nod of their heads. Once they are finished, they take their seats.

"And sitting next to Emma and Rose, we have Travis. Travis is the leader of the Windairians."

Travis follows the same greeting as the Fairley Folk, Emma and Rose, with just a head nod and not much of a smile, then takes his seat.

"Last, but not least, we have Fisher. Fisher's people will not be mentioned during this meeting, as he is here as a favor for the Council."

Before Fisher is able to greet the others, the Ember brothers start making a commotion.

"What do you mean by Fisher's people will not be mentioned during this meeting? How are we expected to sit in this Council Meeting and trust the people here, if we do not know who they lead?" King Preston demands to know.

"Again, who he leads is not the purpose of this meeting. If you feel you are not able to continue with this meeting, which I have called, you and your brother are welcome to leave at any time," the Council Leader replies to King Preston.

"How dare you speak to me that ..." King Preston is cut off by a loud voice.

"Your Highness, please do not question the Council again. My people are of no concern to the Embers. I will tell you this, if you keep pressing this issue, you will find out who my people are as soon as I walk out of this meeting myself. I can promise you, you do not want to have our first meeting to be one of a battle, because I can assure you my people outnumber yours, combined with all the others at this table. Now, if you don't mind, sit back down or walk out of those doors. But if you choose to stay, drop the attitude and disrespect. Do you understand?" It is Fisher who has broken the tantrum of the King of the Embers.

King Preston doesn't like what he is told, but for the first time in history, the other leaders finally see fear in his eyes. The King takes his seat back at the table and does not dare utter another word.

"Thank you, Fisher. Now that everyone has met, let me get started letting you know why I have asked you all here. I have asked you all here because we need help with a very time sensitive matter. We are aware that there are many things each of your people can do that others can't. Now before anyone thinks we called you here to find out exactly what all you can do, that is not the case. We are looking for a specific gift."

"And what special need are you looking for?" Emma, of the Fairley Folk asks.

"I am not sure how much you know about the Council and what we do, but protecting history is one of our duties. Another is protecting the future. In order for us to do this, there has to be a balance between them both, the past and the future.

"And just how exactly do you protect either? What's in the past is the past, and what hasn't happened yet is undetermined fate. There seems to be no way to protect either of them," Travis questions the Council Leader's statement.

"Thank you, Travis, for coming all this way, but we will no longer need your services on this task. I am sorry for wasting your time by having you attend this meeting, but please understand why we can't have you sit in on this meeting any longer. I'm sorry, but you are excused from this meeting," the Council Leader informs Travis.

"You are excusing me from this meeting because of my comment?"

"To put it simply, the answer is yes. You are not going to be able to help us. Again, thank you for coming, and we are sorry for any inconvenience we may have caused you or your people."

Travis stands from the table and makes his way to the entrance, now his exit, doors. That is the last they see of Travis.

"Does anyone else have anything to say before I continue," the Council Leader asks the remaining three leaders. "Well good then, since there are no other questions, I will continue."

The Council Leader continues, "If you are still here, then you are aware that there are ways of protecting both the past and the future. We have never had to ask for help from others before, but it seems that the one we could count on for these matters has betrayed us. We believe she has gone back in time and erased herself from history, and in doing so, she is no longer here with us in our timeline. Her actions are causing ripples along the timeline that have not completely caught up with us, yet."

"What kind of ripples are you talking about here?" King Preston asks in a respectful manner, remembering Fisher's requests.

"We are unsure just how far this one even may branch out. The one who has gone back and erased herself from history is a valuable part of all of our survival throughout the years. She has been able to go back in time, not only to correct some minor things in history, but to change its outcome. Trust me when I say that her missions have been for the good of us ALL. Now, without her here in our timeline, she will not be able to do the good she has done over the years, putting us all at risk of being affected. But we still have time to repair the damage before its ripples reach us. This is why we have no time to waste," Council Leader finishes.

"And you are sure that once you go back in time, if one of us can and will be able to assist you in going back in time, that you will be able to repair the actual timeline? And by repair, I mean not to go back and change things towards your advantage in this current timeline? How do we know that that is not the exact reason the person you trusted went back and erased herself in the first place? Maybe it was because of what you were having her do for you?" To everyone's surprise, it was Fisher who is asking these questions.

"You are going to have to trust us. We would not be telling you any of this if we had any other reason for needing to repair this damage. Now that you know that we have had the opportunity to go back for many years to change anything and haven't, then you should be able to trust us now," Council Leader pleads with the remaining three group leaders. "Again, time is running out. We need to know if any of you, or your people, will be able to help us go back and fix this. And quickly?"

The Council Leader now waits for any suggestions from the three remaining leaders. Emma of the Fairly Folk, Fisher of the Aquarians, and Ember brothers, King Preston and Prince Payton, all sit around the table looking at the other leaders, no one wanting to make the first move to admit they can help with time travel. They all know they can, in one way or another, but to reveal that power in front of the other leaders could lead them into a confrontation later. Everyone remains quiet, until Preston, the King of the Embers begins to speak.

"We can help you, but there will be a large price to pay. You understand I'm sure."

"And what price are you requesting?"

But before Preston can answer, he disappears, leaving Payton as the King of the Embers.

"You were saying your highness?"

"I'm not sure what just happened or what you are talking about."

Little did they know that one of the ripples of the time changes has already reached them in a most peculiar way!

"Where is my brother, King Preston?"

"Who, your highness? You are the King of the Embers. You have no brother to speak of."

"How is that possible? He was just here with us, standing where I am now. Do you not remember him just being here?"

"I'm sorry my Lord, but it has just been you here representing your people," Emma interjects.

"I need a minute to think. Something has happened to my people, or just my brother, but something has happened," King Payton states as he slowly takes a seat.

"Oh no. It has already began. We are running out of time as we just sit here. The time ripples are already affecting us. We need to act now before anything else changes. Now, who is going to help?" the Council Leader asks the group.

"We all are going to help," replies Fisher, leader of the Aquarian people. "Now let's get to work."

Acknowledgements

I would like to thank Rochelle and Nevaya, for allowing me to call their house my home during a time of need. They are truly my lifesavers when I needed one the most. I also would like to thank my family, as always, for being my biggest supporters and fans. Not to mention, characters.

Next, I would like to thank my editor, Patricia, of Carpenter Editing Services, LLC. She has been a second mother to me for many years and with her editing skills, advice, and opinions on *Time Keeper, School Bound*, and now *Search Begins*. Without her, this work of art would not be what it is today. She brings such joy in my writing with her suggestions and honest critiques. Not to mention, her patience with me has been amazing. With my reading disability, she has been able to teach me more about proper English and being able to become a better writer. Along with my Editor, I need to thank my Beta Reader, Jordan Eagles, whose feedback was amazing and helped create this final product.

I would also like to give a quick thank you to the places that allowed me to sit and write in their establishments when I needed that creative energy. A few of those places are Overtime Grill and Bar (off Lakeshore Pkwy in Birmingham, AL), Rose, who is also a character introduced in this installment works at Overtime, Dunkin Donuts (off HWY 119 in Pelham, AL) and 700 Riverchase (in Hoover, AL), Tejano's Tex-Mex (Cooper, TX), Jorden at Bada Bing's (Atlanta, GA). Without these places listed I would have been lost, because as someone with ASD, social settings are not easy for me, and I never felt out of place or any pressure at these creative energy spots. These places made me feel at home every time.

Last, but not least, my fans. If not for you, my words would sit on paper, never to be read.

Continue along with Ian, as he continues to find a way to save his best friend, Kayla, in *Loose Ends*.

Robert Starnes

An Exciting and Adventurous way to view History

Book Four of the

Saving History Series

Loose

Ends

Robert Starnes

Chapter 1

Who Won?

As Jax makes his way from the home he once had with the Believers in North Zulch, he swears he can feel a faint call from Kenzie saying, "Jax, we should have listened to you." Of course he is not sure if it is real or just what he expects to hear from them, Ian and Kenzie. He does not have much faith that they will wait for his return before going into Maria room to look around, even after they said they would wait for him.

Jax could feel the fear in Kenzie's las thoughts to him about Maria having taken Brayden and Connor away from the school. He still can't believe that Maria, of all people, being the Head of the Believers would do something like that. "She is the head of the Believers. No matter her reasons, she is breaking every rule of a Believer and the moral codes of being human," Jax is talking to himself while driving as fast as he can, without breaking the speed limits, or laws.

He does not have to drive too long down Farm Market road 1452, to Highway 190, until he reaches Interstate 45 South, towards Houston. From there he knows his drive will be almost two and a half hours, with traffic. He may not even be close to Houston yet, but he knows there is always traffic in Houston, especially at the time of day he will be arriving downtown at the school.

Kenzie, can you hear me? Jax continues to try to make some kind of contact with her mind as he drives, to give him something to do, and to make sure they are okay, but he receives no replies. He will continue to repeat trying to connect with her mind until she answers, or he gets to school and finds them. Right now, all he can do is drive and keep trying to contact Kenzie.

***

Maria leaves Mason standing there, alone in the conference room, the one they were using in the Control room. As she begins her exit of the Control room, she stops at the door. Her phone seems to be buzzing in her pocket, she reaches for it to see what is so important. Upon retrieving her phone from her pocket, she reads a message on her lock screen that read, "Room Alarm Tripped." That message seems to make her eyes brighten up like the northern star in the night sky at dusk, and a small smile shoots across her hardened face.

"I knew I would catch the other two, once they found out that they were not actually hearing me, nor watching me down in the school lobby. Brayden was right, they did go right up to my room looking for him and Connor. I wonder what too them so long before going into my room? Could it have been due to moral issues, or maybe it is because Jax would not allow them. Either way, I cannot wait to have them as well to add to our collection," Maria says to herself, softly. "Now I just need to get back before anyone notices they are missing as well as the ring he gave Kayla.

Maria makes her way out of the Control room, closing the door behind her. Not too fast or loud to draw any undue attention to herself from Mason, or anyone else in the room. This is one new development that she wants to keep to herself for as long as she can. Or at least until she can confirm it is who she believes she has trapped in her room.

She makes her way down the hallway, with a little more pep in her step that is noticed by one of the guards.

"You must have somewhere important to be ma'am," the guard sounds off to Maria.

Caught off guard, Maria replies, "Excuse me?"

"Well, it's just that you seem to be much happier leaving here that when you first arrived and you are also moving at a much faster pace. You would think you were running to watch an enemy's house burn to the ground, while blocking the roads so the fire trucks couldn't get to it in time," the guard conveys some humor.

"Oh, no. I mean, yes, I am in a hurry. I have to get back to work before people notice I'm gone, that's why I'm walking so fast."

"Yes ma'am. Well, be safe out there on the streets. I hear traffic is something terrible today in Houston."

"It's Houston dear, Traffic is always horrible every day, but I will do my best," Maria ends their conversation so she may exit the building to get to her car and begin her drive to the school, in downtown Houston. She knows it's going to take her about two and a half hours to get from Woodville, with traffic.

As Maria takes her seat in the driver's side of the car, all she can think of is the importance of her finding those two in her room, but she also knows it could be Jax himself. She would prefer Kenzie and Ian, but she would take Jax just as well. She knows that if she has Jax, then none of the children, Kenzie, Ian, Connor, nor Brayden would allow anything to happen to him and do exactly what she and Mason as them to do. So for her it would be a win-win scenario either way.

Maria takes highway 190 from Woodville, but unlike Jax, she is not one to obey the posted speed limit signs or laws. So even though her and Jax has the exact same distance and time to travel, and they have left at the same time, without the other knowing, Maria looks to be the first to arrive at the school, ahead of Jax.

***

Kayla does not fight against her new body guest and allows him to lead her to Mason's office. She keeps thinking this is a very bad idea, but her visitor assures her otherwise. He repeatedly tells her that they are going to be fine, because Mason and Maria are in their meeting, as she already knows, so their coast is clear.

The pair of them head down the hall towards Mason's office, in Kayla's body of course. It does not take them long to reach his office, as it is not too far from her room. He likes to be as close as possible to her at all times.

Now that they are standing in front of his office door, Kayla asks her company, "Now what?"

"Mason is so convinced no one would ever betray him, even after his traitor was revealed, great job by the way, he still leaves his office door unlocked," he replies while reaching for the door knob and giving it a quick turn.

To Kayla's surprise, the door is indeed unlocked. She, or they, push the door open to Mason's office and quickly walked in and shut the door behind them.

"Figures he would have such a large office, and look at all of those books. There must be over a thousand of them. Why in the world does he need this huge oak desk? Who does he think he is, the President of the United States?" Kayla is talking to her partner in crime out loud at the moment.

"To his followers, he might as well be the President. Now, we need to get back to business here. Do you mind if I take control over your body again?"

"Fine, but let's be quick. I really don't want to get caught in here."

The visiting History student from another place and time, takes control over Kayla's body and leads her over to Mason's office safe. The same safe he placed the ring in, the one Kayla gives Ian on his eighteenth birthday, or did give to him already. Without hesitation, Kayla's hand moves to the keypad on the door of the safe and begins to press in a six digit code. The light on the safe turns from red to green, letting them both know the safe is unlocked now.

"How do you know the code to his safe?" Kayla's asks her companion.

"History, remember?" He tells her. "Did you know that safes actually go back to the 13th Century B.C.? The first safe was found in Pharaoh Ramessess II's tomb. It was a wooden safe, can you believe that? But it was made with the same locking system like the ones we use today, with pin tumbler locks. It was built with movable pins that dropped down into hold that would lock the safe door. It wasn't until the mid-19th Century that Charles and Jeremiah Chubb, of England, received the first patent for a burglar-resisting safe and began producing them for others to use."

"No, I didn't know any of that, and I forgot you are a History student. You seem like you study too much. So, what are we getting out of here that is more important than my safety?"

"Trust me, you will soon find out!"

As Kayla's hand turns the handle to the unlocked safe and gives it a quick pull, she notices right off the bat what they are there to take. "We are here for Ian's ring."

"I told you, you would know soon enough. Now we need to get the ring and get out of here, NOW!"

"What are those?"

"What are you referring to?"

"Why would Mason has a lock of hair, a journal, some old coins, and who is in that old picture?"

"I'm sorry, but I can't tell you about those things, we are only here for the ring. The less you know about the future the better. We can't mess up the future, we just need to get it back on the right path."

"Fine, whatever you say. This is your mission anyway. So, are we ready to get the ring and go to my room now?"

"Yes, now grab the ring and close the safe door and press in the code again to lock it back. We need to be going, if my memory serves me correctly."

Kayla grabs the silver ring Alexis gave her to give to Ian on his eighteenth birthday, so this must mean she will be able to give it to him again, but as soon as she touches the ring she freezes.

Kayla? What's going on? Why can't I speak with your voice and why are you just standing here? Kayla's body occupant thinks to her, as he is unable to speak out loud with her own voice.

***

Ian is back in his memory of the skiing trip he took with his fictional family. The one where he has an older brother, Pete, a niece Kourtney, a little brother John Dock and little sister Ashley. He is right back where Pete dropped two large bags at his feet. They are unloading the car after just getting to the cabin before they can go to the slopes. This is the same dream he was torn away from to be lead to the memory of Sebastian and Grayson's fight.

Ian bends down to pick up at least one of the oversized bags Pete has left at his feet, but before he has time to retrieve it and head into the cabin, the cabin and his family disappear again. Ian is back in the white room he knows all too well. He knows this is the same room Junior used to communicate with him before he was wiped from the future, with Kayla erasing herself from History.

Junior? Can this really be you? Jax says he believes it is you, Ian thinks to anyone at this moment. He is truly not really sure what to expect.

Yes Ian, it is me, Junior. I am here with you, but right now you are in a bad situation that I'm not sure I can help you get out of.

What are you talking about? I'm with my family. I am just fine.

No Ian, you are not fine. You and Kenzie are in big trouble right now. You have both been knocked out by a sleeping spell. You are both asleep in Maria's room. We have to find a way to wake you up before she gets here!

I don't understand. I feel fine. I'm happy here. Why would I want to leave?

Ian this is not your life, or even your true actual memory. This is just a dream of what you wish life could have been for you, but it's all fake. You did go skiing, but it was just you, John and Donna, your mom and dad. You have no siblings or even a niece. You are an only child. Ian, you have to remember!

Why? Why do I have to remember? Why can't I just stay here?

You have to WAKE UP and get out of Maria's room NOW! If not for you, then think about Kenzie. She is stuck in here with you!

***

Jax makes his two and a half hour drive from North Zulch in only two hours, thirty minutes before he anticipated. He does not take the time to park his car in the parking garage of the school, but instead he parks right in front of the front doors.

He jumps out of the car and burst through the front doors and ignores the concierge, on a mad dash to the elevators. He is in such a hurry, he does not recognize another student yelling out his name.

"Jax! Can I speak to you for a minute?" The student finally catches Jax's attention.

"Sorry, but I don't have time to talk at the moment, can it wait until later?" Jax replies to the student.

"Okay, but it's about class," the student replies.

"Then you will be fine," Jax concludes their conversation.

Jax jumps into the elevator as soon as the doors open, as he had pressed the call button as soon as he arrived in the elevator lobby. Once he is alone in the elevators he presses the button for the fourteenth floor, as that is the floor for the heads of the faculty, like Maria, stay.

Jax his to endure the hum of the elevator belts and the tick of the digital clock counting the floors as they pass them. The anticipation is ripping him up inside. He knows he has to find Ian and Kenzie before Maria does, and he knows the first place he must look is her room, since he has a feeling they did not wait for him to get back before they went into her room, like he suggested. If they are in her room, he has to get them out before she can get them, if they are to be safe. Then sound the loud 'ding', letting him know he has made it to the fourteenth floor.

As quick as the elevator doors can open, Jax slides between and begins his rush to Maria's room, 1402. He reaches her door, grabs the door knob and give it a twist, and he finds it unlocked. He pushes open her door and finds…

***

Maria skids to a stop at the parking garage entrance, knowing she has already lost precious time due to her being stopped and given a ticket for speeding on her way through Houston. She knows the speed limit signs are there for a reason, and she should have obeyed them. Now she will have to suffer the consequences.

Once she was able to get into the parking garage and park her car, on the third floor, which was the first level with an open spot, she took it. She has her own spot on the first floor, but it seems that someone has parked in it during her absence. She knows she does not have time to deal with that right now, she needs to get to her room. She gets out of her new parking spots and makes a quick step to the elevators in the garage to take her down to the ground level of the structure.

She has taken the elevator from the third floor to the ground floor in the parking garage, and as she steps up to the door, she swipes her card for access, but it is not working for some reason. She continues to try again, but still no access. By this time Maria is furious that she does not have access to the building. She is beginning to worry if she has been found out about working with Mason.

Maria plays it cool and presses the intercom button to get the concierge.

"Yes, may I help you?" Comes the voice from the speaker of the concierge on duty for the evening.

"I am Maria, Head of the Believers, and I reside in unit 1402 and my access card is not working. You can start by buzzing me in and having me a working access card and key to my room before I make it to your desk, there in the lobby. Do I make myself clear?" Maria is still trying to sound the same way she always would, and if she suspects nothing at the moment.

"Yes ma'am! Right away! I'm not sure why your card is not working, but I'm sure it's just a glitch in the system. Your new card and key will be ready as soon as you make it to my desk," the concierge speaks through the speaker as Maria hears the doors being buzzed unlocked for her access.

Maria takes the door and swings it open to make her way to the concierge's desk. "My new card and key please!"

"Yes ma'am. Here you go. So sorry about the mix up at the exterior door. I'll make sure it won't happen again," the on duty concierge replies as she is handing Maria over her new access card and room key.

"Thank you," Maria spouts back to the, now upset concierge, who picked the wrong shift to switch with a coworker. As Maria is snatching the card and key out of her hand.

Maria turns and makes a rush for the elevators. As soon as she reaches them, she presses the up button and has to wait for one of the three elevators that is currently working this evening, which looks to be coming from the Sky Lounge floor.

The elevator stops for her in the lobby, the doors open, and she enters with only one thing on her mind now. Who is she going to catch in her room? So she presses the button with the fourteen on it, for her floor. "I can't wait to see who I have caught this time!"

The elevator stops on the fourteenth floor, with a loud 'ding', and Maria quickly steps out and makes her way down to her room door. Upon arrival, she does not notice anything unusual about it, so she put in her key, unlocks the door, grabs the handle and pushes the door open to find…

About the Author

Robert Starnes is not only the author of *The Multifamily Housing Guide Series: Leasing 101 - Garden Style*, and *The Saving History Series: Time Keeper, School Bound,* and *Search Begins,* but he is also the publisher. He created Starnes Books LLC so he could have full control over his work and to be able to help other self-publish authors with free advice on what they can do to save money and not be taken for their hard work.

After being diagnosed with Asperger's Syndrome, which it is now part of a broader category called ASD (Autism Spectrum Disorder), at the age of 43, things started to click with him. After being able to identify and manage the parts of ASD he had, he was able to hone in on his creative writing. At a young age he did not like to read, because he had difficulty with the words on the pages in front of him. He knew the words and understood them, but his brain would comprehend them faster than his voice could speak them. This would cause him to either leave out words, or cause him to read very slowly so he could have his eyes go back over the words again, two to three times, before his voice caught up with his brain. This embarrassment would stop him from reading for many years.

As an adult learning to face his fears, he began to read John Grisham novels. He loves the law and movies, so it was perfect for him to read the "The Last Juror" before watching the movie. After reading such a great novel then watching the movie, he quickly learned he enjoyed comparing the differences between the novels and movies. That was all it took for him to begin to enjoy reading for the first time. For many years he would only read novels that were going to become movies, because that was what he enjoyed about reading. After many years, he read another novel that became a movie, but they never completed the movie series. The novel was so good that he completed the book series, which in turn gave him a new enjoyment for reading without the novels becoming movies.

With this in Robert's mind, he has written his series for anyone that may be going through the same things he went through as a child, or adult, with reading, and is trying to find a way for them to connect with the world of reading. He believes that you can read and write a perfectly great action packed novel that does not have to be 800 pages thick to be accomplished. He believes giving someone the opportunity and a way to enter the world of reading, then that's the accomplishment. No one should be afraid to read or write in their own style for others to be able to want to read. His mind does not work the same as a traditional writer's does and retains things much more than another person's may, so you will not find very much repeating, or recapping, in his series. You will find action, adventure, and history from the very first chapter to the very end.

To Robert, everyone is different and unique, and should be celebrated every day for being just who they are. He finds that when life may get you down, you can always get away in your own imagination with the help of a good book.

He was born in Texas, but now does most of his writing in Alabama. To learn more about him and his books, visit starnesbooksllc.com, or follow @Starnes_Books on twitter, and find @starnesbooksllc on Instagram.

Books by Robert Starnes

Saving History Series

Time Keeper – Starnes Books LLC (2018)
School Bound – Starnes Books LLC (2019)
Search Begins – Starnes Books LLC (2019)
Loose Ends – Starnes Books LLC (2019)
Final Hour – Starnes Books LLC (2021)

The Multifamily Housing Guide Series

Leasing 101: Garden Style – Starnes Books, LLC (2018)

The Multifamily Housing Guide – Leasing 101 Garden Style Edition – Lulu's publishing (2016 retired print)

Books Published by Starnes Books LLC

Novel Study – Time Keeper *– Patricia Carpenter (2018)*
Trip of a Lifetime *– Eric K. Reinholt (2020)*

www.ingramcontent.com/pod-product-compliance
Lightning Source LLC
Chambersburg PA
CBHW050138110726
47898CB00008B/2575